MW00636031

FOREVER WILDE IN ASTER VALLEY

LUCY LENNOX

Copyright © 2021 by Lucy Lennox

All rights reserved.

No part of this book may be reproduced in any form or by any electronic or mechanical means, including information storage and retrieval systems, without written permission from the author, except for the use of brief quotations in a book review.

Cover Art: Natasha Snow Designs

Editing: One Love Editing

Proofreading: Lori Parks and Victoria Rothenberg

Beta Reading: Leslie Copeland

KEEP IN TOUCH WITH LUCY!

Join Lucy's Lair
Get Lucy's New Release Alerts
Like Lucy on Facebook
Follow Lucy on BookBub
Follow Lucy on Amazon
Follow Lucy on Instagram
Follow Lucy on Pinterest

Other books by Lucy:
Made Marian Series
Forever Wilde Series
Aster Valley Series
Twist of Fate Series with Sloane Kennedy
After Oscar Series with Molly Maddox
Licking Thicket Series with May Archer
Virgin Flyer
Say You'll Be Nine
Hostile Takeover

Visit Lucy's website at www.LucyLennox.com for a comprehensive list of titles, audio samples, freebies, suggested reading order, and more!

AUTHOR'S NOTE

Dear Reader,

Some of you might remember that Miller Hobbs was the young man who showed up on Grandpa Wilde's doorstep and made the connection between the Marian and Wilde families. But for those who need a quick recap (like me):

1. We first met Miller in *His Saint* when he showed up on Grandpa Wilde's doorstep claiming to be related based on a DNA test.
2. We heard a little more about Miller in the end of *Wilde Love* when the Wildes met the Marians at the vineyard and Tilly and Grandpa reunited.
3. We learned much more about Tilly's backstory, including Miller's relationship to the family, in *Made Marian Mixtape*. In order to refresh your memory, you're invited to download the story "Poker Face" here for free.

However, you do not need to remember any of these events to enjoy this story. I've tried to write it in such a way that your memory will be tweaked by little contextual cues in the narrative, but if not, simply insert "nosy family member here" when you see a name you don't recognize. If you want a cheat sheet, there's a family tree/list at the end of the book.

Enjoy the Wilde ride!

Love,

Lucy

P.S. Thank you to my husband for giving me a little "Raine space" to write this book. And for coming up with the phrase in the first place.

P.P.S. Thank you to May Archer for giving me the motivation as well as the feels needed for this book. Since the book was pretty much her idea, many thanks are needed here. Feel free to thank her, too, by *picking* up one of her books. Pun intended.

1

MILLER

"Take him down, mother... fudger!" Ginger Marian screamed at the giant television screen, loud enough for the Riggers players to hear her in Los Angeles.

I was starting to believe this special football-viewing room had been the key selling point to the Marians' rental of Rockley Lodge in Aster Valley for the family reunion in the first place. Not only was it large and filled with comfortable leather recliners, but it was also decorated with priceless NFL memorabilia owned by Tiller Raine, the celebrity quarterback who apparently owned the lodge itself. And the acoustics were...

"Yeah!" Ginger's shout echoed around the room, and she jumped to her feet to perform a kind of rhythmless bump-and-grind that made the baby girl in her arms—a baby I was almost positive didn't belong to her and my cousin Pete—shriek with contagious laughter. "Tackle him! Eat dirt, Nelson Evangelista! Isn't that right, Reenie?" she cooed at the baby, who laughed even harder.

"So I told him no," Nico Wilde continued as Ginger and the baby kept dancing. "I refuse to ink any version of a spider, even if it is a cartoon one. That's too creepy. Find someone else."

"That's hardly fair," Ben muttered, absently rubbing his calf through his blue jeans. "Some spiders are sweet."

Ben was my cousin Griffin's biological brother, and I was pretty sure he was married to the tall guy named Reese, who was outside with some of the Wilde cousins. I knew for sure that Ben had a memorial tattoo of his daughter's tarantula right at the spot he was rubbing, though, because he and the other guys had been showing off their ink the day before, and that experience had been *seriously* memorable.

It turned out I had a thing for guys with tatts. Who knew?

"Pfft," Nico replied. "Your tattoo is the only exception and only because you're my best friend's baby bro. And… okay, maybe if Georgie wants her own one day, I'll do it. But only because no one else is touching her virgin skin."

The Marian and Wilde men sitting around him collectively shuddered at the idea of anyone even thinking about inking one of their precious, perfect babies.

It was kind of adorable.

"*Holding*!" Ginger shouted. "Blatantly holding! Come on. Is that ref sleeping? Jesus help us."

Nico's daughter climbed off his lap and walked over to Ginger to pat her knee with a chubby toddler hand. "Jesus can't help," she said, knowingly. "He's a bad man."

West choked on his beer and sputtered. "Pippa, baby, who told you that? That's not true."

Ginger lifted an eyebrow of accusation at West and Nico. "I thought Texans loved their Jesus."

"They do," Nico assured her. "I mean, we aren't churchgoers ourselves, but we aren't haters either. I don't know where she got—"

Otto Wilde blurted, "Jesus fucking Christ, is this ref *insane*?"

Pippa nodded and shot a sympathetic glance at Ginger. "See, Auntie Ginge? Told you. Jesus is a bad man."

Ginger bit her tongue to keep from laughing while West buried his face in his hands and Nico sighed.

"As I was saying," Rebecca Marian said sweetly, pulling me back to her earlier conversation while ignoring the antics of her daughter-in-law and her... *Huh*. What relation were Nico and West to Rebecca, exactly? My brain throbbed just trying to piece together the complex relationships there. "You have to use the hand mixer because stirring it with the whisk doesn't break up the clumps of sugar well enough. It will make the chocolate sauce lumpy."

I nodded even though there was no way I'd retain any of this information.

My senses were completely overloaded, and I felt a horrible headache coming on, and that was before I even started processing all the emotional baggage of finding out that I was part of a huge family I hadn't known existed. While I could tell the Marian and Wilde families were made up of very good people, and I knew just how lucky I'd been to learn I was related to them through that DNA registry last year, being in the midst of so many new faces and personalities was exhausting and over-whelming.

I was an only child of an only child sitting in a room over-flowing with new-to-me cousins. There were at least twenty of them, and that didn't even include their spouses or kids, my biological grandparents, grand... *uncles*, and all the various friends they'd brought with them on this holiday vacation to Colorado.

Not for the first time in the seven months since she died, I wished my mom was with me. It had been just the two of us for so long, but she would have *thrived* in a situation like this, and it felt strange enjoying it without her. Now, despite the crowd of loving family around me, I felt a little... lonely.

The idea behind the trip was very kind. The Wildes and Marians had wanted to meet up somewhere to get to know each other better and welcome me into the fold. Now that my mom was gone, this crazy crew was all I had left, and I barely knew them.

"We're going to fix that," my grandmother had said with a firm jaw and determined glint in her eye. Tilly—because god forbid I call her Grandma—was a force to be reckoned with. When she set her mind to something, it happened. And when

3

she'd heard that I was planning to spend the first Christmas since my mom's death alone, I'd practically seen the wheels turning in her brain.

Which was how I ended up sitting between all these gorgeous men with a bowl of popcorn in my lap and a life-sized cutout of a famous football player staring at me from the corner of the room.

"I'm not much of a cook," I told Aunt Rebecca. "But I've always wanted to learn."

She wasn't technically my aunt, but I'd learned early on that the Wildes and Marians played fast and loose with familial endearments. I kind of liked it. I'd never had aunts or cousins, so it was fun to try it on for once. Trying it in a setting like this, though, was a bit like taking a toddler's training wheels off and dropping him in the Tour de France.

She smiled and nodded. "It's tough when you work as much as you do. You'll need to make an effort to take some time out for yourself. Tilly said she worries about you. It's one of the reasons she was desperate to go away instead of hosting the reunion in California. Not that I would have minded visiting you down in Monterey. It's so beautiful there."

I ignored for a moment the strange concept of Tilly worrying about me. Rebecca was right about my work schedule, and it wasn't the first time someone in the family had mentioned it. There had been several special occasions the Marians had invited me up to San Francisco or Napa for that I'd had to decline because of a work commitment.

I hadn't realized that being the marketing director for a regional orthodontics chain would require such long hours, but I'd been wrong. The only reason I'd been able to take time off for this trip was because I'd appealed to my bosses' old-fashioned sense of family obligation.

But the overworking I'd been doing lately was also due to my need to take on some side projects to pay off debt my mom had left behind. The extra work was definitely a contributing factor to my stress levels peaking right now. I'd come into this trip to

Aster Valley already exhausted and overwhelmed, so being among this many new people put me over the edge.

"I think I'm going to turn in early," I said to Rebecca. "Unlesss…" I glanced over at a card table in the corner of the room, where my grandmother was playing cards with Harold, Irene, and Granny. "Unless you think that might upset Tilly? I don't want her to think I'm avoiding everyone or being antisocial."

Rebecca's expression softened, and she leaned over to pat my arm. "She'll understand. Everyone had a long day of travel to get here. Don't forget, she and the girls came yesterday with Dante and AJ and stayed at AJ's parents' house. I'm sure that's the only reason she's still up. If she'd traveled today with the rest of us, she'd probably be heading to bed early, too."

I thanked her and stood up, hoping to sneak out of the room as if I was just wandering to the men's room. The last thing I wanted to do was bring attention to myself, especially since I seemed to be the first adult to call it quits.

As I headed toward the door, though, laughter broke out in the corner of the room, and my eyes strayed toward the card table again.

I'd only known my grandmother for a year or so, and I still didn't know what to make of her. Sometimes when she smiled or lifted her eyebrow in a snarky way, she looked so much like my mother that I couldn't help but love her. Other times, though, my feelings were… more complicated.

We'd done the ancestry DNA test because one of my mom's bucket list wishes after learning of her terminal lung disease had been to find her birth parents. I wasn't sure what I'd expected to happen when we'd gotten our DNA matches, but I definitely hadn't been prepared to have Tilly ignore my mom's attempts to reach out for weeks and weeks.

When she'd finally come around, which had only happened after I'd tracked down Grandpa Wilde and he'd convinced her, Tilly had explained to my mother and me the whole story of how she'd come to put my mother up for adoption. Hearing about her unplanned pregnancy at age eighteen by a young Harold Cannon

—long before he'd become a senator and fathered a United States president—and how her family had sent her off to a home for unwed mothers and taken her choices away, it was hard to resent her for any of the decisions she'd made in the past.

But seeing the strong, confident woman she was now, a woman with plenty of financial resources, a loving family, and even a second-chance romance with Harold, it was hard to understand why she'd hesitated to get to know her dying daughter. Why she'd wasted months she could have had with my mom.

She's trying to make up for it now, I reminded myself. *That's why you're here.* And I was going to try to let my resentment go, too. My mom would want that.

I stopped at the card table to kiss Tilly on the cheek. "I'm heading to bed. Can I get you anything before I go?" I said in a low voice.

"If he's slipping you the ace of spades, I'm calling bullshit," Granny snapped. "Son, step away from the table right now and show me your hands."

I stepped back and turned my hands back and forth like I was a dealer in Vegas. "All clear. Promise."

"Mpfh," Granny mumbled before frowning back at her hand.

"Besides," I added, pretending to sneak a peek at Granny's cards, "How could I slip it to her when it's already in your hand?"

Irene tittered, and Granny let out a squawk of indignation until she realized I was teasing.

After Tilly laughed and shot me a wink, and my grandfather gave me an approving smile and a handshake, I left the room feeling a little happier. It wasn't that I was uncomfortable with the Marians. Not at all. In fact, it was impossible to feel uncomfortable with people so kind and welcoming. I'd been around them in smaller groups several times since being reunited with my mother's biological family, and I liked them a lot. It was the sheer quantity of people in the same place all talking over each other and demanding each other's attention that got to me.

I did better one-on-one.

The large lodge was quieter outside of the TV room. I made

my way upstairs to the main level, where I could hear the clink of dishes coming from the kitchen. I poked my head in and saw our host, Mikey, hard at work washing dishes.

"Can I help?" I offered, moving over to the counter where a dry towel lay next to a stack of wet plates.

"No need. You're our guest here. I usually have help with this part, but the young lady we hired to help us out has a bad cold, and I don't mind stepping in. Besides, it keeps me from worrying about Tiller while he's playing."

"Tiller's your husband, right? The football player?" I asked, grabbing the towel and a plate despite his protests. I loved feeling useful.

Mikey brightened. He was a cute guy with a friendly demeanor and had been very welcoming to all of us so far. "Fiancé. He plays for the Houston Riggers. They're in Los Angeles for a game tonight. He's recovering from a hamstring strain, and I know he's probably fine, but it's better for me to stay busy and away from the television until I get the all clear. I can watch the game after I know he came through it okay."

"Ginger—my, um… cousin—is a football fanatic. I think she would actually faint if she saw him in person."

He chuckled. "Then we'll have to keep an eye on her when he gets here tomorrow. They have a bye week this coming week, so he'll be able to come spend a few days here."

I joined him in his laughter. "Oh my god, she's going to flip. My grandmother and her friends will probably flirt with him. They're incorrigible."

"I don't mind as long as everyone knows he's mine at the end of the day," he said with the same quiet confidence my cousins had when talking about their relationships. For the briefest moment, I let myself imagine what that would feel like to have someone like that in my life.

"What about you? Are you dating anyone?"

Reality came crashing back. I shook my head and reached for another plate. "I don't have much time for dating. My job is demanding and—" I hesitated. I usually didn't share too much about my personal life with people I didn't know well, but Mikey

7

had been nothing but kind, so I continued. "My mom was sick for a long while, and I was helping to take care of her. She passed away over the summer."

"Ah, man. That sucks. I'm sorry for your loss." Mikey gave me a look of genuine sympathy.

"Thanks. I do sometimes wish I had time for dating. But don't tell anyone in my family I said that. They're notorious matchmakers, and the last thing I need is to be set up by my fifty closest family members."

After I stacked the dry plate, Mikey handed me another. "My family is the opposite. They weren't very supportive about my being gay, so their idea of setting me up involved lots and lots of women."

I groaned. "I'm sorry."

He grinned. "It was fine, actually. I made quite a few good friends that way. Besides, I think if I'd still been single when I moved to Aster Valley, it would have been worse. My friends here are just as bad, and they're mostly gay guys. I'm not sure which is worse."

"Is there a good community here?" I asked, mostly just to make conversation. I was enjoying his easy company and the coziness of the kitchen.

"Really good," he said sincerely. "A gay couple owns the local diner, and they latched onto us right away. Introduced us to a ton of other guys. We have a pretty good group now. I'm sure you'll meet most of them this week while you're here. A few of them promised to help us decorate the lodge for Christmas. Our friend Truman has been making homemade garlands for the mantels and bannisters, and his partner, Sam, has a crew of guys coming to put lights on the lodge. He's in charge of all the facilities and physical operations of our ski resort. And Tiller's friend Julian will be in town through the holidays, too." A worried expression flickered over his face before his sweet smile reappeared.

"And that's… a problem?" I guessed.

"What? Oh, no. Not at all. I love Julian. He's a wonderful guy and a brilliant attorney. He's just been a little…" Mikey hesi-

8

tated. "Unlucky in the love department. Hey, are you *sure* you're anti-matchmaking? Because I wonder if—"

"I'm positive," I assured him quickly. I had enough to handle keeping up with my work, getting my debts paid off, and navigating my way through my new family. Romance, even with a brilliant attorney, was *not* on my to-do list.

We talked a little more about the ski resort they were opening in another month, and I learned they were deliberately keeping it low-key for the first season in hopes of ramping up slowly and preparing for a larger launch the following winter. Mikey was easy to talk to, and before I headed off toward my room in the south wing of the lodge, he made sure I knew he was available to talk to anytime.

"I know what it's like to feel like the odd man out," he said softly. "Even though I can tell from the looks on everyone's faces downstairs they adore you."

"Did someone tell you my story?" I asked. I didn't mind—it wasn't like my mom's adoption and my recent inclusion in this large, extended family was a secret. But I was surprised since we hadn't been here a full day yet.

Mikey turned off the sink and turned to me, reaching for the towel in my hands so he could dry his own. "Your grandmother told me a little bit about it. She was worried about you. Said she wanted to make sure you felt welcome and had some space to yourself to get away from the noise."

I smiled. "Tilly's not afraid to share her opinions, but she can also be very kind and thoughtful," I said. It was one of the things that made my feelings toward her so complex. "But… yeah. It's a little overwhelming. I mean… I'm really glad to be here, but it's very different from what I'm used to."

"I think it's cool that you found your mom's biological parents like that. I can't even imagine what it must have been like to realize you came from a giant family of…" He stopped and blushed.

"Influential politicians? Talented musicians? Actual royalty? Mostly gorgeous gay men?" I suggested with a smirk.

"*Yes*, that one." He blew out a breath and clapped a hand over

9

his heart. "Holy cow. I think Tiller is going to freak out when he realizes I've been hosting the cast of *Magic Mike* while he was away."

I laughed. "To be fair, he gets to be in the locker room with dozens of pro football players."

Mikey swatted my leg with the towel. "Hush. I don't want to think about it."

"Don't you, though?" I teased.

Mikey stepped over to the large double fridge and pulled out a bottle of water. When he handed it to me, he thanked me for the help with the dishes.

"I'm really glad you're here," he said. "If you need any help settling in, please let me know."

"If you need any help while your assistant is sick and Tiller's away, please let me know. I'd love a chance to be helpful, especially if it gives me a break from the crowd."

He nodded and thanked me before sending me off to my room. After spending several hours trying and failing to fall asleep, I finally fell into a fitful slumber for a little while. I awoke before six in the morning and stumbled out to the kitchen in search of coffee.

Mikey was already up and looking as bleary-eyed as I was.

"Is your offer to help still valid?" he asked.

"After I get this cup of coffee down, it sure is."

With the address to the local bakery programmed into my phone and the keys to Mikey's SUV in my hands, I made my way out into the frigid December morning to pick up the special order of breads and pastries Mikey had ordered for breakfast. I loved driving down to the valley as the earliest bands of warm pink sunlight washed across the tips of the mountains on the other side of Aster Valley.

This part of the Colorado Rocky Mountains was beautiful, and the town itself was quaint and quirky, with unique shops and restaurants making up the small downtown area. I found a parking spot on a side street and walked up the shoveled sidewalk to the bakery. A large plate-glass window revealed the baker himself kneading a giant blob of dough on a well-worn wooden table in the back of the shop.

Something about the sight stopped me in my tracks and caused me to watch him a little longer than I should have. A little longer than was probably polite. Maybe it was the rhythm of his movements or the fact he seemed to be talking to himself. Maybe it was the way he fit the landscape—solid as the mountains, warm as sunlight, simple and magnificent at the same time. Maybe it was the way his big hands kneaded the dough with such total competence that shivers danced up my spine. Whatever it was, I couldn't look away.

After standing still a few moments, I realized he was singing. He had headphones on and nodded his head to a silent beat. The man's face broke into a wide, white grin as his hips began to sway, and his whole body moved with the music as he went about his work.

The baker had a messy brown bun on top of his head and a short beard with dark brown eyebrows over an expressive face. I wondered idly if he had dimples I couldn't see from this far away. His smile was breathtaking.

He looked to be around my age, mid-to-late thirties, but it was hard to tell through the window. He wore a denim button-down shirt under a beige apron sprinkled with flour. The rest of him was hidden by the table.

I couldn't stop watching him. I felt like a kid outside of a candy store with sticky hands pressed to the glass and big eyes filled with want.

I liked to think I was a fairly practical sort of person, a person who made the best of what he *could* have and didn't spend his time yearning for things he couldn't, but the baker had me captivated.

This one, a voice in my head whispered as I watched the baker's biceps bunch and flex under his shirt. *Yes, please.*

"You have to try the melomakarona," a woman said from behind me, startling me out of my weird, lusty fantasy. "I can't believe this place hasn't been overrun with people clamoring for it. It's only a matter of time. Or… it would be if they'd do a little advertising or start a mail-order business for them. The only other place I know of that had Greek treats as good as these was a bakery I went to once in Chicago when I was in college. That place had people lined up around the corner this time of year, just to get the melomakarona."

I turned to face the stranger, finding it harder to look away from my baker—*the* baker, I silently corrected myself. *The* baker, who was in no way mine—than I could have imagined. The woman was bundled in a puffy purple jacket with a gray wool hat over blonde hair and had a baby strapped to her chest. She smiled at me way too brightly for this hour of the morning.

"What's melomakarona?" I asked politely.

"It's a Greek Christmas cookie made out of honey, walnuts, and orange juice. You have to try it. Come on," she said, grabbing my elbow. "I'll get you one."

I couldn't help but laugh when I realized I'd left my own meddling family just to find myself being woman-handled and managed by someone else's, but I was more than willing to go along with any scenario that got me closer to my—*the*—baker. "Okay, if you insist. I hope they have good coffee, too."

"Definitely. And they also do an incredible kourabiethes cookie that melts in your mouth. The only reason I let myself come here so often is because I'm nursing. Surely that earns me some extra calories to spend at the bakery, right?" She continued her friendly chatter as she led me around the corner to the front door.

When we entered, I immediately felt at home. The warm space was extra cozy with an old brick fireplace in one corner and deep, comfortable-looking sofas and chairs clustered around it. Holiday music played softly from hidden speakers, and it was noticeably different from whatever up-tempo beat the baker himself had been playing in his headphones. The air was fragrant with sweet cinnamon and a dozen other spices I couldn't name but wished I could.

A young woman smiled from behind the counter. "You're up early, Tessa. Is Hoss teething again?"

The lady who'd brought me into the shop groaned. "The

baby's name is Conley, dammit, Hannah," she said with a laugh. "Don't listen to his Uncle Declan. And yes, he's teething, so he's been up for hours. It was a good excuse to come grab what I wanted before the crowds turn up and take all the good stuff."

I had no problem believing that they'd sell out quickly, considering how tempting the pastries looked and smelled. But I was still focused on something far more tempting than sweets.

While the young lady behind the counter began filling a bakery box, I moved to the side to try and catch a peek through the arched doorway into the back of the bakery.

I could hear the clank of metal sheet pans, and I spotted a glimpse of the baker's denim sleeve rolled up over his thick forearm. His thick, *tattooed* forearm.

Oh, man. Tattoos, too? *Hngh.* My palms went sweaty, and I had to swallow past a lump in my throat. I was a sucker for a man with ink.

I tried to tell myself firmly that this baker was none of my business. That I didn't know a thing about this man. That I was a tourist, for heaven's sake, and I was already dealing with a ridiculous number of new people in my life on top of all my work stress at home. But none of it seemed to matter. Something about this total stranger called to me, and I was dying to get a closer glimpse of him.

2

DARIUS

I normally tuned out everything going on around me when I was baking, but for some reason, I noticed the man outside the window this morning. He stopped and stared as if mesmerized by something as simple as kneading bread.

He was pretty cute, if a little more clean-cut than the men I usually dated. Blond hair and a button nose, navy blue peacoat rather than a true parka. I wondered if he was a tourist rather than a local. Had he been local, I probably would have noticed him before. There was something about him... something memorable.

Maybe it was the sad eyes. There was pain there, and I couldn't stand seeing someone else in pain. But I also couldn't very well take on the burdens of strangers on the street, no matter how lovely and compelling I found them to be.

I fell into the rhythm of the upbeat music in my ears and tried to tune everything out.

But I couldn't tune him out no matter how hard I tried.

It had been a long time since a man had caught my attention. After my relationship of four years had crumbled under the weight of a growing business back east, I'd sworn off dating for the foreseeable future. I hadn't had the time or energy to right what I'd done wrong with Clay, namely not have time and energy for my partner.

But now it had been six years since Clay had left. Six years of casual encounters and keeping my distance.

I debated long and hard before deciding that maybe I could take a chance just this once. Smile at the man in the window and see what happened.

But of course, by the time I looked up, he was gone.

"Darius!"

I jumped and yanked off my headphones at the penetrating sound of Hannah calling back from the front counter. "Yeah?"

"Customer has a question for you."

I quickly stopped by the sink to wash my hands before making my way up front. The blondie from outside stood next to one of our regular customers. Was this her husband? I'd never seen her with anyone, but it made sense there was a father for the baby she usually had with her.

A flare of disappointment hit my gut. *Oh well.*

The woman smiled her usual friendly smile at me. "I was trying to tell this man... I'm sorry, what was your name?" she asked, turning to him.

So, not her husband. Better. In fact, excellent.

"Miller," he said softly. "Miller Hobbs."

"Right. So I was telling Miller to come back later for the hortopita special. He asked if it was different from spanakopita."

Hannah shot me a smirk. She knew how much it bothered me when people mistakenly called my hortopita spanakopita only because that was the more common type of Greek savory pastry. She could have easily answered the question herself, but she knew I liked to educate customers on the difference. I couldn't say I minded a chance to talk to the man.

Miller.

"Yes," I began. "They're similar but different. They are both made with phyllo dough, but spanakopita is made with spinach. Hortopita uses mixed greens with a focus on the herbs. I source my herbs from a local spice merchant who grows them here in Aster Valley. Since I can get the freshest herbs and greens for it, it's like being able to offer a taste of Aster Valley in a savory pie."

Hannah looked smug. The lady with the baby looked excited. And Miller Hobbs looked like a deer caught in headlights.

"What do you like, Miller?" I asked in a low voice. "Sweet, savory? Pastries, cakes?"

Our eyes met, and I let out a breath.

This man will be someone important to me.

I didn't know how I knew it, but I did. My whole body relaxed in a way I'd never experienced before. I should have felt nervous, excited, maybe even a little freaked-out, but I didn't.

I felt ready. And patient.

He caught his bottom lip with his top teeth as his eyes flicked to the display case.

I wanted to feed him. I wanted to present everything in my arsenal to him like a peacock unfurling his feathers.

What do you like? I wanted to repeat it until he answered, until I knew every single way to make him happy.

"I like... honey," he said, and a gorgeous blush turned the tips of his ears red.

Hannah chuckled, and I felt my cheeks stretch into a Cheshire grin.

"Then you've come to the right place," I said. "Wait here."

I returned to the kitchen and began packing up a bakery box for him, quickly followed by a second box. Samsades, diples, loukoumades, and a gorgeous apple tart with rosemary and honey syrup. I also added some of the molasses clove cookies popular this time of year and a couple of pieces of chocolate cheesecake brownies because I hadn't met anyone yet who didn't love them. It was enough food for ten people, but it didn't feel like enough.

When I came back out to the front of the shop, the woman with the baby was gone, and Hannah was bagging up a large call-in order from Rockley Lodge.

"I put together some things for you to try," I said, handing the boxes to Miller. "You'll have to come back and let me know which ones you like."

"Wow, you… you didn't have to do this. I…" He glanced up at me, unsure. "How much do I owe you? This is amazing."

"No, nothing. On the house," I said, suddenly feeling embarrassed. It was a little over-the-top as random gestures to strangers went.

I was surprised when Hannah took the boxes from him and placed them in the same bag with the big Rockley Lodge order.

"I can't let you do that," Miller said, reaching for his wallet.

"I insist. Really. Are you staying up at the lodge?" I asked, desperate to change the subject. Hannah was going to grill me later. The reality of my unexpected behavior began to sink in.

"Yeah, uh… it's like… a big family reunion kind of thing." He pinned his lip with his teeth again. "I guess Mikey wanted to make sure we had plenty of sweet treats to go with breakfast."

He wasn't the only one suddenly feeling insecure. I'd heard through the small-town grapevine that Mikey and Tiller were hosting at least two dozen beautiful gay men at their lodge this week. I'd thought it was a joke at first, but now…

I cleared my throat. "Well… good. That's good. You'll have plenty of people to share your extra pastries with."

We stood there awkwardly while Hannah moved over to help a customer who'd come in behind Miller. I wasn't ready to let him go, but I didn't know what to say to keep him there.

"Can I help you take that to your car?" I offered, nodding at the two giant bags of bakery boxes.

He offered me a small smile that lit up his eyes and made my heart speed up. "That would be great. Are you sure you don't mind? I'm only down the side street right here. Not far at all."

We walked out of the warm bakery into the frosty morning.

"You're going to freeze," Miller said. "You don't have a coat."

"Nah. I'm from Chicago. This is nothing."

He led me around the corner and down the side street to an SUV I recognized as Mikey and Tiller's. After we put the bags in the back, I opened the driver's door for him. "How long are you in town for?"

When he moved past me to get into the car, I caught a whiff of soap and coffee, a unique combination that probably also carried a subtle addition of my bakery now, too. I found that idea soothed some primitive part of me I hadn't known existed until Miller walked into my bakery.

"A week. We're spending Christmas together. It's…" He blew out a breath. "Kind of a big deal. But also… stressful."

"Too much family?" I offered, knowing full well how that could be. My mother was from a giant Greek family, and my father was from a very large Black family. I had aunties and theias, uncles and theios. Grannies and yayas. More cousins than I could ever visit in my lifetime. They were spread out all over the world now.

Miller nodded. "It's overwhelming. I'm an only child, and so was my mom. But then we found her biological family and… it's like…" He let out a soft laugh. "Enormous. And truly… unbelievable. They're wonderful, and very welcoming. But I'm not used to being around so many people all the time, especially people who are trying so hard to include me in everything. And… well… my mom died earlier this year, so it's… weird."

I wanted to pull him into a big bear hug, but that sounded like the opposite of what he wanted. And since he didn't know me from Adam, it would have been completely inappropriate anyway. The vulnerability in his eyes gave me the impression that he didn't share much about himself, especially his burdens, easily. So, how could I help ease his burden another way?

"I'm so sorry about your mom. What an amazing gift she gave you before leaving, huh? A big nosy family. A blessing and a curse, if you ask me." I tried to keep things light to ease his burden rather than asking him to expose his heart to a stranger. "First of all, the trick with a big family of busybodies is to dish their shit right back. They hassle you? Hassle them right back. Stand up for yourself and claim your space. They'll respect you for it."

"I'm not exactly the hassling type," Miller said with a sweet smile.

I grinned right back. I couldn't help it. "No, I don't imagine you are. What you need, then, are some activities that keep everyone busy. Idle chitchat while you're doing something else is much easier to handle than sitting around being interrogated by well-meaning family members."

"We're going Christmas tree shopping today," he said. "Apparently there's a Christmas tree farm nearby."

I nodded. "I haven't been out there yet, but I've heard great things about it. It's on a ranch, and the rancher offers horse-drawn sleigh rides, too. Are there any little kids in your group?"

"A few. They'd love that. Heck, I'd love that. Thanks."

"There's also the ice rink over in Steamboat. And you can ask Mikey to be sure, but I think they have the main ski lift running now even though the slopes aren't open yet. There's a log road you can hike down. And if your crew is more into doing stuff indoors, there's a great used bookshop down the street that has a board game room in the back. What else?" I tried to think, which was hard to do with Miller's big eyes staring up at me in something like wonder.

He reached out tentatively to brush a clump of flour off my apron, but his fingers rested over my pec for a second longer than strictly necessary. Time seemed to stand still for a beat. I clenched my hand against the desire to grab his and pull him into an embrace.

"And, uh..." I continued, trying to focus on anything other than the brush of his masculine hand over my chest. "Art galleries? There's a paint your own pottery place next to the library. I haven't tried it yet, but... but I've been meaning to. And, um..."

My phone beeped in my pocket. I fumbled to pull it out and noticed a text from Hannah asking for help packing up another large catering order.

"I'm sorry," I said. "I need to get back in there, but... will you promise to come back and let me know what you think? About the pastries, I mean?" I realized too late I was just another person putting pressure on him. "Or not. Whatever makes you happiest. Have fun, okay?"

His face was flushed pink from the cold, and his sad eyes were a little brighter. He was stunning.

"Thank you..." he said, lingering as if trying to recall my name. I realized I'd never given it to him.

"Darius," I said. "Darius Grant. It's nice to meet you, Miller."

His smile was radiant. "You too."

When I returned to the bakery, I jumped right back into work. We were slammed with holiday and catering orders like the one from Rockley Lodge, which meant Hannah and I didn't stop moving until we closed at three. Instead of jumping right into prep for the next morning's baking, I went to the gym in time to join a kickboxing class. It was just what I needed to work out the jittery feeling I'd had all day.

On my way home, I got a call from my mom.

She always opened with the same line. "Why are you avoiding my calls?"

It felt good to laugh.

"Because you deliberately call me in the morning when you know that's the busiest time for me. And we both know you do it on purpose so you can leave a voicemail and get credit for the call."

"That's my lunch break at work," she said with fake indignation. "My boss is very strict with personal phone calls, as you know."

"I've heard she's a raging tyrant," I teased. The road up the mountain to my house was dark, so I paid close attention to the edges where an animal could dart out at any time. "You should quit."

"Then who would run this shitshow? No. It's better that I stay. No one else could do it the right way."

Even though she was joking, we both knew there was truth to her words, and she wasn't the only one in our family who felt that way. When I was in elementary school, she'd developed a software program for use in human resources departments. It had taken off so quickly, I'd grown up as one of "five kids," where the fifth child was my mother's growing company.

I'd inherited her entrepreneurial spirit as well as her controlling tendencies, but where she thrived on the cutthroat corporate world, I'd felt suffocated by it. After spending a decade growing my original Chicago bakery concept into a national chain with my parents' encouragement, I'd finally learned an invaluable lesson. It was okay to choose happiness over corporate success.

"Delegating isn't a four-letter word, you know," I told her. "You might at least consider giving Selina more responsibility on the financial side." My sister was already a VP at the software company my mom owned, but she was desperate to do the financial analysis work she'd gone to business school for. It was hard for Mom to let go and see Selina as a capable businesswoman rather than her little girl.

"Believe it or not, I met with her just this morning and handed over the reins on all the financials. She is officially the CFO of MomTech as of today."

I grinned at the company nickname my siblings and I had started using years ago. "That's great news. Congratulations to the both of you. No wonder you called me. You're probably using it as a distraction to keep from yanking all your files back from Selina's greedy hands."

"Hush. I didn't call to talk about me or your sister. I wanted to see how it's going there. How are you handling the holiday rush?"

I threw the truck into Park and sat looking out at the frozen branches in the trees in front of my driveway. The bright light from my headlights made everything eerily beautiful. Winter was never this "clean" back in Chicago. It reminded me of a winter wonderland.

"Handling it just fine. We took some of our usual products off the menu and replaced them with the holiday treats. That worked well. The cookie decorating classes were amazing. Even though they made for a long day, it was a nice way to get out and meet people, just like you said. I have my last one this week, but I think I'll offer it again around Valentine's Day."

"You can always hire someone to do that part for you," she suggested absently. "Spend that time back at the shop filling more orders."

"Mom," I barked, trying to get her attention back. "Why would I do that? Do you remember why I left Chicago?"

She sighed. "To break your poor mother's heart?"

"Mm. Close. To get away from a life that wasn't making me happy. Working that hard wasn't making me happy."

"And are you happy now, kamari mou? So far away from everyone and everything?"

I stepped out of the warmth of the truck and into the starry night. When I turned to walk to the house, I caught a glimpse of the view of the valley past the glass-and-steel house. Lights from town sparkled in the crisp, cold air, and this far above the main thoroughfare, there wasn't even any road noise. The mountain around me was silent.

I pictured the sweet man I'd met earlier at the bakery. Miller Hobbs. His perfectly tidy clothes and his sad eyes. His radiant smile and sexy blond hair styled just so.

"Yeah, Mom. I think so."

She paused for a beat. "Sounds like there's something you're not saying."

I laughed as I let myself into the house and turned on the lights. The view was still there, only now it was across the room and through the wall of glass in my living room. "There's a lot I'm not saying."

"You know… your sister ran into Clay last week. Said he asked about you."

I thought of my ex's habit of showing up when he found himself between relationships. Over the years, there had been several times he'd turned up for a "quickie for old time's sake." After saying yes the first time and then seeing the disappointment on his face when I'd left to go to work, I'd sworn off ever doing it again. He may have said it was casual, but he hadn't meant it.

"I hope he's well," I said, meaning it.

"He looked good. It made me wonder if… well, now that you presumably have more time, maybe you could give things with Clay another chance. I'd like to know you had someone there to take care of you. A mother worries, you know."

I walked through the living room to the wall of windows. The opposite side of the valley was too far away for me to identify a

22

specific building, but I could guess where the lodge was by its proximity to the empty expanse of the ski slopes.

Miller is over there right now.

Was he sleeping? Probably way too early for someone who didn't work the hours I did. Were they drinking and having fun? Swapping family stories and playing games?

"You don't need to worry about me, Mom," I assured her. "I told you I'm happy. I met a cute guy today and made him smile. That made me happy." I shook myself out of the trance I was in and tried to cover up that mom-bomb with other news. "I also delivered a birthday cake to a woman in a nursing home who turned 100. Can you believe it? And the sweetest little girl was in my kickboxing class tonight with her mom. She was killing it."

"Go back to the cute guy," she said, never missing a beat. "And tell me everything."

"There's nothing to tell." *Yet.* "I promise when there's something to tell, I'll let you know."

She made a *tsk* sound. "I noticed you said 'when' rather than 'if,' so I'll hold you to that."

After she made a big point of asking me to call on Christmas Eve when all the family would be gathered, we said our good-byes. I made my way back to the bedroom and stripped down in anticipation of a long, hot shower.

As soon as I stepped under the hard spray, I let the image of Miller flood my mind again.

Even if I didn't see him again, it felt good to have been so drawn to someone, to have made him smile when he'd been feeling a little blue. This kind of sparked interest was one of the reasons I'd sold my previous business and moved to Colorado the year before. I wanted a life again, time to be someone outside of work, to have friends and lovers, adventure, time at home.

I wondered what it was about Miller Hobbs that had sparked such a reaction in me.

After the rest of the evening speculating, I came to zero conclusions, but I knew one thing.

I wanted to learn more. Much, much more.

3

MILLER

My cousin Simone knew something was up the minute I walked into the kitchen back at the lodge.

"You're blushing," she accused. "Something happened."

"It's cold outside," I countered, blushing even harder. "I challenge you to go out there and not come in with red cheeks."

Her brother Jude snickered into his coffee while he lay snuggled up against his much larger husband's side. I still couldn't believe I was related to *the* Jude Marian. The first few times I'd joined the family at group dinners, I'd had to forcibly stop myself from staring at him.

But then he'd farted on purpose right when his brother Blue was trying to make a toast to his husband on his birthday, and Jude's brothers and sister had made such a big dramatic deal of how disgusting he was, I'd laughed too hard to ever take him that seriously again.

"Where'd Miller go?" Simone asked Mikey, who was busy setting out more coffee mugs on the large island. "Who would have been there?"

"Leave him alone," Tilly said, entering the room looking like she just stepped off the cover of a Growing Old Gracefully magazine. She wore a luscious ivory sweater and charcoal-gray slacks. A diamond-and-emerald broach in the shape of a wreath was pinned to a rose-colored cashmere scarf around her neck.

I gave her a grateful smile and then stuck out my tongue at Simone. "Yeah, what she said."

Simone's surprise quickly morphed into a teasing grin, and she shot me the bird while her brothers hooted in support of me.

I blushed even deeper. I'd done as Darius had said and dished it right back. Even though I was sweating in the spotlight of everyone's attention, it felt kind of good to be part of the teasing instead of watching it from the outside.

Mikey grinned supportively right before he betrayed me. "I sent him to Honey's to pick up some pastries for breakfast. The baker there is a total hottie. His name's Danny."

"Darius," I corrected without thinking, tasting the syllables on my tongue. The name was alluring and familiar, strong and sweet, just like...

"*Darius*," Simone and Jude singsonged back, and only then did I realize my error.

I bit back a groan. This was going to be excruciating.

"A hottie? Is that right?" Doc asked from his spot in a comfortable chair by the windows. Nico and West's one-year-old lay on his chest and fiddled with a button on his shirt. Grandpa —who was actually my great-uncle but had invited me to call him Grandpa anyway—sat in a chair next to them and fed Doc a sip of coffee every few minutes so he didn't have to take his arms away from little Reenie.

"We like hotties," Grandpa said, shooting me a wink. "Tell us more."

"Yeah, tell us more." Cal Wilde nodded enthusiastically while his older partner, Worth, rolled his eyes.

"Don't encourage them, Calgary," Worth muttered under his breath, hooking a finger into his husband's belt loop to draw Cal closer to his side. The two of them sat nursing their own coffees at the kitchen island while several of the Marian cousins sat at the kitchen table doing the same.

"Nothing to tell," I said, reaching into one of the bags to help unpack the bakery boxes. "Other than the fact you're going to love the stuff in these boxes. I've never seen such gorgeous pastries. He... I mean my... I mean *they* seem to specialize in Greek recipes, and he... *they* packed some samples for us."

"Is the baker nonbinary?" MJ asked in a whisper.

Her wife, Neckie, who was in the middle of plucking the baby off Doc's chest, answered, "I think that's Miller's way of acting like the bakery is a large, random group of non-hotties rather than a singular Greek hottie. Isn't that right, Miller?"

I tried ignoring them, but they were the least ignorable people on earth.

Mikey produced three large serving platters for us to spread the pastries out on. I placed one on the kitchen table, one on the island, and took the other over to the kitchen seating area by the fireplace. Everyone groaned with pleasure as they dug into the treats.

Thankfully, the subject changed to the plans Dante and AJ had made to take all of us Christmas tree shopping. Mikey had given us permission to decorate our own tree in the sunroom, and Tilly planned on surprising everyone with a personalized ornament to put on it while we were here. All we had to do was pick out the perfect tree and some strings of lights.

Dante's excitement was contagious. "AJ's mom says they do nighttime sleigh rides, so I signed us up for some later this week. Teddy said he'd take some family pictures in the snow, too. I think we should all coordinate what we wear."

My heart pinched at the mention of AJ's mom, and just like that, a wave of grief hit me. Even after seven months, a seemingly minor thing—a stray word or a song lyric, even the scent of a perfume that smelled like hers—would remind me that my mom was gone.

I obviously didn't begrudge AJ his parents and in fact was looking forward to meeting them since they lived here in Aster Valley—but it hurt regardless.

I forced myself to take a deep breath and return Dante's excited smile the way my mom would've wanted.

"I kind of love the idea of family photos," I ventured.

Griff groaned. "I feel like we're always dressing matchy-matchy for family photos." His husband, Sam, walked up and kissed him on the cheek.

"As long as I can see some of your ink in the final shots, I don't care what you're wearing in the photo," Sam murmured before nuzzling Griff's neck. "Mornin', Fox. You snuck out of bed before I woke up."

Griff wrapped his arm around Sam before stealing his coffee mug to take a sip. "I took advantage of Tiller and Mikey's workout room in the basement. That thing is killer. It has everything."

I made a mental note of another excuse I could use if I needed a break from family time. Work out in the gym. Hopefully, I wouldn't be too intimidated by whatever impressive setup a pro footballer had down there.

The conversation continued around our plans for the day as the rest of the Marians and Wildes trickled into the kitchen in search of coffee and breakfast. Mikey finally shooed us all out to the much larger dining room, where he'd filled large chafing dishes with crispy fried potatoes, scrambled eggs with fresh herbs, crusty homemade bread still warm from the oven, and a peppered pecan bacon that smelled incredible.

By the time everyone finished praising his cooking talent to the skies, Mikey was flushed and happy, which was how his fiancé found him only a few minutes later.

"Honey, I'm ho-ome!" a deep voice called from the front hall.

Mikey's eyes widened in surprise for a split second before he went tearing out of the room to greet Tiller. The giant athlete was already in the doorway to the dining room when Mikey ran into his arms at full speed.

They embraced like they hadn't seen each other in months, which might have actually been the case. With Tiller's game schedule and Mikey's preparations for our big visit, it wouldn't have surprised me if they'd been apart for several weeks.

When their welcome home hug turned into a welcome home make-out session, my cousins began cheering and calling out scores. I couldn't help but laugh, and once I started, I couldn't stop. Despite having a decent group of guy friends back home, I'd never been in such a fun, welcoming group as this one with so many examples of healthy relationships. It was easy to let the affection in the room wash over me, and I wondered, not for the first time, if it would ever be my turn to find something as special as many of my cousins had found.

After a giant round of introductions during which Ginger almost fainted from fangirling and Hallie, one of the middle Wilde sisters, almost fainted from Tiller's sheer hotness, we settled down to finish the big breakfast. I took the opportunity to glance around at all of the faces of my new-ish extended family.

You would have loved this, Mom.

I swallowed the lump in my throat and dug in.

&

"Finally, a true white Christmas," Charlie said, holding his hands out to catch the few flakes coming down as we exited the passenger vans at the Christmas tree farm. "Not many white Christmases in Ireland. The most we get is a dusting."

Hudson held out the gloves Charlie had forgotten in his haste to exit the van. "Put these on, or your hands will be white, too," he warned.

Charlie's long red hair blew around his face, and his grin made his eyes bright. "As if you know snow any more than I do, Hudson Wilde."

"We get snow," he said defensively.

"Pfft," Hudson's sister Sassy said, flitting past him with her bright-red scarf wrapped snugly around her neck. "Hardly. And you lived in Dallas for several years, remember? It rarely snows there at all."

"Back in my day," Grandpa began, but the rest of his story about walking uphill in snow both ways to school was drowned out by the sound of everyone within earshot groaning. Doc looped his arm through Grandpa's and leaned his head against his husband's shoulder.

"Don't worry, sweetheart. I'll listen to your boring old stories any day of the week."

"Mpfh." Grandpa grumbled before turning to press a kiss against Doc's forehead.

As I watched everyone spread out to assess the lay of the land and head down different paths through the trees, I realized Darius had been right about another thing. It was much easier to handle all of my outgoing cousins when we were engaged in an activity.

"This way," AJ said, leaning in to speak softly enough that no one besides Dante and me would hear. "I know the secret stash of perfect trees."

I followed them all the way down the path past row after row of trees. The light snow flurry was just enough to make the Christmas tree farm a little magical but not too much to make it hard to see. Like Charlie, I hadn't experienced white Christmases either. I'd grown up in California, and my time in the snow had been kept to irregular visits to Tahoe for skiing.

This was vastly different from the larger town of Lake Tahoe. Aster Valley, including the ranch with the Christmas tree farm on it, was nestled in a narrow valley between two mountain ridgelines. The eastern side held Rockley Lodge and the ski slopes, and the western side supposedly had more private residences. Without the vast expanse of the lake, Aster Valley seemed somehow cozier and more intimate than Tahoe.

What I'd seen so far of it, I'd really liked. I wondered what it would be like to have one of the houses on the mountainside that looked out over the valley below. AJ's family lived in a house like that, and Tilly had mentioned the view. I imagined how small we would look from above, meandering slowly among the trees.

"Dadddeeeee!" I recognized the child's scream from off to my right. It was a sound of terror coming from Jude and Derek's son. All of us went running in that direction, imagining the worst.

When we got to the row where Wolfe was now sobbing into Derek's neck, we realized the source of the little boy's fear. Someone very large was dressed up as Frosty the Snowman, and the costume was disturbingly menacing on such a large person. Clearly, the person in the suit was horrified they'd scared little Wolfe, so they tried apologizing and patting Wolfe's back which only scared the kid more. "I'm sorry, buddy. I didn't mean to frighten you."

"Get the fu—*uh-udge* away from him," Derek growled at the overgrown snowman.

Jude became the peacemaker. "We'll take care of it from here. He's just easily overwhelmed by large... cartoon... characters."

Granny wasn't so polite. She took her handbag and swung it around at the snowman's fluffy white ass. "They're telling you to fuck off, Snowy. Get lost. Who the hell scares the bejeebers out of a kid like that? Psychopaths, that's who."

Dante leaned over to whisper in my ear. "I've never been able to figure out why she'll use the f-word one minute and then a word like bejeebers the next."

I bit my lip against a laugh.

The snowman suddenly seemed to notice he was surrounded by at least thirty adults related to the child he'd inadvertently scared. He began backing away slowly with his paws up. "Easy... easy now. I only smiled at him, I swear!"

"Sam? What's this I hear about you having a surprise for..." An adorkable young man in a bow tie came hustling over to the scary snowman. He took in the scene with a single glance and shot us a nervous smile of apology. "Oh. Oh, wow. Babe, when I suggested tapping into my costume collection for later, I was thinking more *gladiators*."

The snowman rolled his eyes to the sky. "Now you tell me."

"Sam... I mean *Frosty*... means well, I promise," Bow-tie-man assured us. "He just doesn't understand that when you're as tall as he is, a snowman with a big smile looks less like less like Olaf from *Frozen* and more like well, a terrifying, man-eating yeti."

"Truman's right. I'd never intentionally frighten a kid." Sam the snowman sounded remorseful.

"No harm done," Derek said grudgingly as Wolfe peeked his head out and smiled.

"Let's go home, baby," Truman suggested, patting Sam's arm. He lowered his voice just slightly. "I'm not sure I've ever told you this, but I kinda have a *thing* for terrifying, man-eating yetis."

Sam snorted. "Is that so?"

"Mmhmm. I'll let you scare the pants right off me," Truman assured him.

Once he'd hustled the snow menace away from the children, we all scattered again to find the perfect tree, even though there was an unspoken agreement little Wolfe would be the one selecting the tree today. Thankfully, his dads helped make sure it was the right size for the spot Mikey had designated.

After an incredibly long family portrait session, we returned to the lodge to discover a large spread of lunch foods and hot drinks set out for us.

I helped fix plates for Granny and Irene, who had to have been tired from all the walking and waiting in the cold, and then I got myself a bowl of shrimp and grits along with another piece of homemade bread.

Once I'd eaten it all, I secretly wondered if it would be appropriate to claim nap time. For the sake of the older ladies, obviously.

But as everyone finished their meals, I somehow ended up with little Reenie in my arms. She was rosy-cheeked and adorably dead asleep, which meant I didn't dare even breathe for fear of waking her. Nico came over to check on his daughter, crouching down in front of my chair and brushing a wisp of hair off her forehead.

"Sleeping babies are perfection," he said softly. "It almost makes up for being hellions when they're awake."

"She's pretty sweet," I agreed. "And I noticed your other daughter is really good with her."

Nico's lips turned up in an easy smile. "Most of the time. Pippa has her horrible moments as all three-year-olds do, but we're pretty lucky. Sometimes I look at the girls, and I still can't believe I'm a dad."

I glanced across the sunroom sitting area to where Nico's

husband West was helping Grandpa string the tree with lights. Instead of untangling the strands, West was watching Nico with a look of adoration on his face. It made my stomach tighten with envy.

"You're really lucky," I said without thinking.

Nico looked up at me. The snakebite piercings in his lower lip were sexy as hell, and I wondered if I'd ever get used to being around so many beautiful, engaging men without feeling like I was in a store full of forbidden candy.

"Luckier than I ever imagined," he admitted, turning to find West in the crowd. They shared an intimate look that made me avert my eyes. When he turned back to me, he tilted his head as if studying me. "What about you?"

I barked out a laugh loud enough to make Reenie stir in my arms. "Shit," I whispered, rocking her gently to lull her back to sleep.

"She's fine. Tell me why you laughed."

I shrugged. "The Wildes and Marians make it look so easy, you know? Like you can just go out there and find your person and live happily ever after. It's not like that in real life."

I hadn't meant to sound so negative, but it was true. My friends back home in Monterey lamented how hard it was to find a man who wanted a committed relationship. I wasn't the only one who was discouraged by the hookup culture around us.

"Agreed," Nico said with a nod. "I lived in the Bay Area for a while and enjoyed the hell out of my time there, getting with whoever I wanted to whenever I wanted to. I always joke that when I was ready to settle down, I had to leave San Francisco and move to a tiny Texas town to find my gay picket fence."

I rolled my eyes. "Exactly. Explain to me how one tiny town in a red state can have an absurd amount of good gay men in it. I've half considered moving to Hobie at this point."

Nico moved to the seat next to mine and sat down. "The thing about small towns is their ability to put two people together over and over again until you pretty much have to get past being cordial acquaintances. With West... well, let's just say Hobie is so small, I couldn't get the fucker out of my face."

West had moved closer until he could overhear Nico's words. His eyes danced with teasing light. "You wanted me in your face."

Nico reached out and flicked West's thigh. "I definitely did not. Meddling know-it-all." He turned back to me. "My point is... you have to get past the anonymity and shallow phase with the people you meet, and that's the hard part. Because when you make yourself vulnerable, you leave yourself open to disappointment. But being vulnerable is how you create intimacy. It's a double-edged sword. You should try it."

I nodded and tried not to think about Darius. The beautiful baker's engaging smile was hard to forget, and if I was going to practice small-town vulnerability with anyone, I wanted it to be him. There'd been something... comforting and easy with him. It wasn't like being around the Marians and Wildes. Being with Darius had felt... like I could let my shoulders down and exhale. Not that he didn't also make my stomach tighten with an excited kind of attraction, too, because he totally did.

Maybe he'd be a good person to practice on since I'd never see him again. I could go back to the bakery the following morning and... what? Try to create intimacy while he was working his ass off baking during the holiday season?

Don't be ridiculous, Miller.

I sighed. Surely, the man didn't need to be the subject of my social experiment when he was trying to run a business. Besides, I was still in mourning for my mother. I still felt like I was in the bottom of a deep dark well that seemed nearly impossible to climb out of some days. And the idea of dating someone she'd never get to meet felt... not wrong, exactly, but weird.

"Sound too daunting?" Nico asked with a chuckle. "That's an awfully big sigh."

I flashed him an apologetic sigh. "No, it's just... I met a guy, and I thought... well, it doesn't matter. But I think you're right. I need to get better at getting past the small talk. I don't really know how, though, without sounding like a bumbling fool."

Saint looked up from the box of ornaments he was sorting

through on the floor near West's feet. "Bumbling fools are pretty fucking sexy if you ask me."

His husband, Augie, blushed deep red and elbowed him lightly.

"Preach," AJ said from closer to the Christmas tree. Dante made a disgruntled noise in his throat.

"Mmhm," Grandpa added, shooting a wink at Doc, who sat in a chair nearby.

Doc crossed his arms in front of his chest. "I've never been a bumbling fool in my life."

"I seem to recall a time several decades ago where you came across me and a ranch hand... *conversing*... in the barn. You bumbled your way into my... *heart*... pretty damned quick after that."

"He means pants," Gina muttered under her breath. "And the two of you are dirty, dirty old men. I know because I was there."

Doc sat up straighter in his chair and pinned his grown daughter with a glare. "I beg your pardon, young lady. You most certainly were not there when he... when I... when we..."

"Conversed?" West suggested with a snort.

"Bumbled?" Saint guessed.

"Besides," Doc continued, ignoring them both, "your mother approved of Major, Gina. She adored him."

Gina came over to Doc and kissed the top of his head. "I know that, too," she said gently. "And so do I. We couldn't have been happier when Pop got into your... *heart*."

Doc laughed and pretended to push her away. I looked around the room and realized just how much love was packed into the sunny space. No, I didn't truly feel like one of them yet, but I couldn't deny they were willing and welcoming enough to be ready for the time when I was.

I readjusted Reenie in my arms and stared down at her chubby face. One day I wanted what Nico and West had. Family, love, parenthood... maybe even owning my own business one day.

And if my daydreams the rest of that afternoon included one

inked-up Greek baker covered in flour and sugar, nobody needed to know.

And if my fantasies much, much later that night in the privacy of my own room moved on to licking that flour and sugar off said baker... well, no one needed to know that either.

4

DARIUS

Miller was back. My heart jumped into my throat when I saw his nervous peek through the archway from the shop to the kitchen.

It was so early, the shop wasn't even open yet. Hannah must have seen him outside and let him in. I'd lit the fire in the fireplace at least an hour ago, so the seating area would be plenty toasty by now.

"You here for Mikey's order again?" I called through the archway, yanking off my headphones.

He held up his hands as if to stave off an attack. "No, no. I mean, yes, I am, but no, I know I'm early. Don't... you don't have to have it ready or anything. I just... I couldn't sleep, so..."

I grabbed a towel to wipe my hands on and hustled around the large table to the archway. "C'mere," I said, gesturing him back to the kitchen. There was no need for him to be nervous, and I wanted to put him at ease as quickly as I could. "I could use your help with something."

Hannah's eyes widened from where she stood putting money in the cash drawer. I never needed help in the kitchen. In fact, back in Chicago, I was notorious for biting the head off anyone getting in my space while baking. But things were different today. First of all, I was no longer in the cutthroat environment

36

of the big city. I'd left it for this very reason. I'd hated being angry and stressed all the time. I'd sold off the big chain of bakeries I'd built and started Honey's so I could get back to enjoying the process of baking.

Secondly, this was Miller. I couldn't think of someone I more wanted in my space than this sweetheart.

He cautiously made his way around the bakery counter and through the archway. I guided him to where I'd been sifting powdered sugar over stencils on a batch of flourless chocolate cakes.

"I have twenty cakes that need sugaring, but several dozen cookies are ready for decorating, too. Would you mind helping me while we wait for Mikey's apple turnovers to finish baking?"

Miller's eyes widened. "This is the shape of a snowflake. It's so intricate and... well, pretty. How did you come up with it?"

I gestured to the sink, where we both needed to wash our hands. "Unfortunately, I can't take credit for powdered sugar stenciling, although I did design this particular snowflake. We have several stencils we use. We have ones with our logo on it in multiple sizes."

After we washed our hands and found him an apron, I showed him how to place the stencil and shake the sugar over it. I could tell he was nervous, but I assured him any mistakes he made would simply mean cutting that cake into sample bites for our customers.

"It's fine," I said, trying to reassure him. "I always make extra just in case."

While he began sugaring the cakes, I got to work decorating cookies across the big table from him. Even though there were a million questions I wanted to ask him, I could tell he needed a little time to get used to his process before being up for conversation.

After a few minutes, he was the one to break the silence. "I just realized what you're doing."

I glanced at the cookies I was working on. "I cover them all with a royal icing base before adding the rest of the —"

He laughed, and it was the best sound I'd ever heard in my

kitchen. "That's not what I mean. You're distracting me with an activity to make conversation easier."

I grinned at him. "I didn't do it intentionally, but I guess you're right. Is it working?"

"It's unnecessary," he said. "You're easy to talk to. Besides, you're only one person. Not nearly as intimidating as a roomful."

"Yeah? Because I want to ask you a million questions," I blurted.

"You do?" Miller looked up at me in surprise. A dusting of sugar puffed into the air above the shaker as he turned to face me. "About what?"

Heat flooded my face. I tried hiding it by focusing back on the cookies in front of me. "Everything. What you like, what you don't like. What you do for a living. Where you live. Who your friends are." I swallowed and asked the one question that might make the others less relevant. "If you're taken."

Another puff of sugar blasted between us as the shaker fell onto the table. Miller cursed and scrambled for it, grabbing it before it had a chance to mar the cakes nearby. His frantic apologies danced between us, tipping through the fragrant air until I was giddy with them.

"It's okay," I assured him, coming around the table to his side and removing the shaker from his hands. After I set it safely down, I reached out to brush some of the powder off his cheek. "I didn't mean to put you on the spot," I said softly as I spent a little too much time making sure his skin was free of the sugar.

I could smell the scent of something fresh and clean coming off his skin, strong enough to be a cologne. Was it possible he'd taken special care this morning before coming here?

I needed to know the answer to my last question.

Miller met my eyes. "No. That is... not... not taken. I'm not. Taken." He swallowed. "But I..."

I brushed my thumb across his full lower lip before moving my hand down to brush some of the sugar from the apron over his chest. It wasn't necessary—what were aprons for if not to catch dust and crumbs?—but I couldn't keep my hands off him.

"You what?" I asked. I begged him not to say something like,

But I have a crush on someone else. Or, *But I'm not interested in being taken by the likes of you.*

"I live in California."

I nodded, trying not to smile at his ridiculous obstacle. It was ridiculous because the distance of a thousand miles would never be enough reason to keep me from something I wanted.

"Mm," I said, stepping back and nodding. I needed to give the poor man some space. He didn't seem the type to want a nosy Greek stranger in his face. "Now I have answers to two of my questions." I moved over to the sink to wash my hands again. "What about a third? What do you do for work?"

Miller let out a breath and reached for the sugar shaker again. "I'm the marketing director for a regional chain of orthodontist offices. I buy media placement like airtime for TV commercials and radio spots, billboards, that kind of thing. And I do some other marketing jobs on the side."

I returned to my spot across the table and took up the royal icing again. "Why do you sound less than enthusiastic about it?"

He placed the stencil on the cake and shrugged. "I love marketing. It's what I went to school for. But when my mom got sick, I left my big corporate job in LA to take care of her. The job I have now was my best option to stay in marketing but also work normal business hours. Now that she's gone…"

Instead of trying to jump in and finish his sentence for him, I bit my tongue and waited. I wanted him to be comfortable sharing his feelings with me, and I was more than willing to be patient. The soft melody of holiday music filtered back from the front of the shop, and I could hear Hannah moving trays into the display case.

My patience was rewarded when Miller sighed and set the sifter down again. "I just don't know what I want to do next. I don't want to move back to the city and have a high-pressure job, but while my current clients are a smaller business, they're so disorganized that they create more work for me, and I end up busy all the time anyway. Plus… I have so many ideas for how best to market my clients' practices, but my clients are too old-fashioned to let me do most of the things I want to try."

"Like what?" I asked, beginning to dot the cookies with colorful icing to make strings of Christmas lights in a zigzag pattern.

"E-commerce and social media, mostly. Their business is perfect for it, but the decision-makers are old dudes who don't get it. They think a nice ad in the Sunday paper is the way to go. It drives me batshit."

"So they aren't letting you be the subject-matter expert in your field."

Miller looked up at me in surprise. "Yes. That's exactly right and an excellent way to phrase it. I guess it makes me feel ineffectual and stuck in the dark ages."

"That doesn't seem like the kind of place that would allow for career growth and fulfillment," I added.

He let out a soft chuckle and went back to his job. "Thank you. Hearing it out loud helps." I couldn't tell if he was being sarcastic or not, but he quickly added, "I mean it. Talking about it like this makes me realize I need to make a change. I'm not happy there. And with my mom gone..."

"Happiness is important," I said, meeting his eyes. The recent loss of his mother explained the sadness in them.

As I watched him, Miller's cheeks and the tips of his ears turned pink, and my attraction to the man zapped me right in the chest. He was sexy as hell and so damned sweet. It was a potent combination, especially now that I knew he wasn't involved with someone.

"It is. So... what about you? Are you happy? Um, with work, I mean? Owning your own place? This is yours, right? I'm sorry. I shouldn't have assumed." He was adorably polite, and the fact that his manners got more formal when he was nervous was incredibly endearing.

"Honey's is mine, yes. I opened it earlier this year."

Miller focused on sifting sugar. "How did you wind up in Aster Valley from Chicago?"

Something inside of me warmed at the realization he recalled our conversation from yesterday, like maybe it had meant something to him, too. "A friend I met in culinary school got married a couple of years ago in Steamboat Springs. When I came to the wedding that summer, I fell in love with the area."

"You didn't like living and working in the big city?"

I never really knew how to explain my previous business to new friends. Whenever I tried it, I either came off sounding like a braggart—*I owned the largest chain of small bakeries in the Midwest*—or a fool—*And I sold it all in hopes of starting one not quite so successful as the last...*

"It was too cutthroat," I said. "I didn't like the pace, and... I didn't really like who I was there."

Miller nodded immediately. "I understand. That's part of the reason I don't want to move back to LA. It's hard not to get swept up in the success competition. I worked so many long hours at my corporate job, I didn't even know what a work-life balance was. Watching my mom die... well, maybe it sounds cliché, but it reminded me that life's too short to live for your job."

"I agree," I said before putting down the last cookie and swapping out the tray of decorated ones with a new tray of blanks. "I really like it here. It's small enough to be relaxing but big enough to sustain the bakery and offer a variety of residents and newcomers, especially now that the ski resort is opening back up. I wanted to find a place where I could be happy at work and outside of work. So far, so good." Aster Valley was slowly coming to feel like home.

As we continued to work, Miller told me what he'd learned about the resort from Mikey and Tiller, and I shared my thoughts on the exciting changes that had been happening around town since my arrival earlier this year. We talked so easily and comfortably, I didn't realize how much time had passed.

"Darius!" Hannah called from the front. "Mrs. Tenley wants to know when you're making cannoli cake again."

I glanced up at Miller to excuse myself for a moment and noticed him yawning. "Are you getting enough sleep?" I asked before moving to the sink to wash my hands. It hadn't been the first time I'd noticed him yawn.

"No," he said with a self-deprecating laugh. "Maybe it's because I'm in a strange bed, or maybe it's the stress of being around people all day. I don't know. But I feel a little like the walking dead."

"Grief is exhausting," I said softly. "And it's probably taking its toll in many ways."

He met my eye, and our connection hung there warmly for a beat. "Yeah," he said finally. "Sometimes it feels like it will never end."

"Not end maybe, but get more bearable." I squeezed his shoulder before moving through the archway to greet one of our regulars. "Good morning, Nori. I anticipate having the cannoli cakes back in January. Right now, we have so many holiday specials, I can't find room to fit them in, too. But you might like the bourekia. It uses some of the same ingredients, but it's a pastry instead of a cake."

After helping her make a selection and thanking her for coming in, I made my way back to the kitchen in time to see the look on Miller's face when he noticed the time. "Oh god! They're waiting on me for breakfast at the lodge." He looked up at me in panic. "Darius, I'm so sorry. I didn't mean to stay so long. Are you okay with me leaving? I was supposed to bring the pastries in time for br—"

I grabbed his upper arms and shushed him. "Of course I'm okay. Not that I want you to leave. You're welcome here anytime. I'll call Mikey and tell him I waylaid you. He'll understand. They're good guys."

His shoulders dropped. "I was having such a nice time here, I completely lost track of time."

Our eyes met, and yet again, I had the swooping sensation in my stomach. Yaya's voice in my head was insistent. *When you meet your person, you're going to know.*

My heart rate picked up. "Can I take you to dinner?"

Miller's lips turned down in a frown. "I don't think .. I mean, we have all these family things planned, and I... I think it would be rude to duck out, don't you? Wait, don't answer that," he said with a self-conscious chuckle. "But... would it be okay for me to

42

come help you tomorrow morning again? I liked this. Talking and baking. It was really relaxing."

I gently squeezed his arms before letting go. "Absolutely. I would love that. Come as early as you want, but if you're sleeping, let yourself sleep, promise?"

He grinned again, and I couldn't help but do the same. "Promise," he said.

I spent the rest of the workday high on the memory of having him in my space, of learning more about him, and even holding his arms in my hands. He seemed to be at a crossroads in his life which was exactly where I'd been a year ago, and I wanted to find a way to support him while he tried to determine the best path forward.

Oh, who was I kidding? I wanted to steer him toward a particular path.

My path.

Because everything in me was confident Miller Hobbs was my person, and all that was left to do was convince him I was his, too.

5

MILLER

I raced back to the lodge, feeling giddy from my time with Darius. He'd asked me out! And he'd invited me back into his kitchen to help him with his cakes. Starting the day with his easy company had helped settle my nerves, but as soon as he'd asked me to dinner, I'd low-key panicked.

Going to dinner wouldn't be like sharing a baking task with him. I'd have to be charming and engaging. What if I talked about orthodontia all night? Or the challenges of negotiating airtime in the Monterey-Salinas media market? No. He'd inevitably find me boring as hell. One of the downsides to being around my Wilde and Marian cousins was realizing how dull my life was by comparison.

Case in point: my cousin Felix Wilde had arrived late last night with his husband, who just so happened to be the king of Liorland—yes, the actual *king* of a country in Europe—and their family. Felix himself was everything that was kind and welcoming, and honestly, so was Lior. But it was hard to be myself around someone who had the equivalent of secret service agents around him at all times.

It was one thing to treat Jude Marian—a Grammy-winning country music star—as a regular person, but quite another to try

44

and be chill around a man whose royal ancestry went back hundreds of years.

"He's just a dude," I muttered to myself as I walked into the lodge with two big brown paper bags from the bakery. "So am I. Normal dudes. Being the marketing director of Happy Teeth is almost the same thing as being the ruler of a small country."

"I assure you, it is not," Lior mumbled, shuffling across the front hall in nothing but flannel pajama pants.

I stared at him while suddenly dying of mortification.

"Mostly because my job is probably considerably more boring than yours," he added. He scratched his stomach idly, and I almost salivated. The man had been voted the world's hottest royal for a reason.

"Sir," his valet, Arthur, said, following him with a burgundy robe draped over one arm. "If you wouldn't mind covering up your... self. You're not in the privacy of your own suite anymore."

"Need coffee," Lior said, turning back and forth as if trying to determine where the kitchen was. "You said I had to get it myself."

"Presumably after dressing, sir," Arthur said with a sigh. "It's unseemly."

"Miller, help me," Lior begged. His hair stood up every which way. "Where is the coffee? And why do you smell like cookies?" His sleepy eyes brightened slightly. "Do you *have* cookies?"

Arthur looked at me. His impeccable grooming and fastidiously pressed clothing was typical for the proud valet. "Forgive him. I forced a sleeping pill on him during the flight last night, and it seems to have created other problems."

"Babe?" The shouted endearment came from down the hall, quickly followed by one of the Wilde cousins, who stopped short when he reached the valet. I tended to mix up Max and his brother Jason, but if he was smiling at Arthur and calling him "babe," this was most likely Max. "Mom wants to know if we packed navy blue sweaters. Don't ask me why. I told her you didn't let me near the packing, so I'd have to ask."

"Yes," he said, reaching out a hand to smooth a wayward lock of hair off Max's forehead. "She wants Teddy to take some engagement photos of us in the snow while we're here."

Max's face turned pink. "Oh. Yeah… good. That's nice. I'd… I'd like that."

Arthur's face softened as he looked at his fiancé. "I thought you might. They'll be better than the ones we had taken at the palace. You looked terrified in those."

Max walked into Arthur's embrace and tucked his face into Arthur's neck. "Sometimes I feel like a peasant in that place."

"Same," Lior muttered before walking off in search of his coffee. "So much same," he called over his shoulder. I followed him to deposit the bags from Honey's.

Mikey looked up with a big smile on his face. "There you are. I thought maybe you'd been kidnapped by a gorgeous Greek man."

My face ignited, but I hoped it could be excused away by my frosty trek outside. "Nope. Just lost track of time, that's all. What's the plan for the day?"

"I believe some people are going shopping in town and some are staying here to wrap presents," Mikey replied. "Which activity you choose is primarily based on how far in advance you planned for the gift exchange." He winked at me and tilted his head toward Granny.

"Zip it, tiny child," Granny snapped. "Some of us are known for our spur-of-the-moment creativity. You can't squash a lady's Joyce de Veeverer."

She butchered the pronunciation of the phrase, which made Cal Wilde spit out his coffee and his partner, Worth, murmur, "I think I went to school with someone by that name," at his plate of eggs.

"It's called joie de vivre, Granny," Tristan said, gliding into the room with masculine grace as if he wasn't carrying one child on his shoulders and another on his forearm. "It's French for poor holiday planning skills."

Granny swatted Tristan's thigh as he walked past her to deposit his kids at the long kitchen table. "Stay," he commanded the two girls. Their metaphorical halos stopped spinning the minute his back was turned. They scrambled down and snuck over to paw through the Honey's bag I still held.

I snuck a cookie to each of them and warned them to sneak back to the table before their dad caught them misbehaving.

"Yes, Uncle Miller," Ella said politely. The kids were used to calling everyone "aunt" and "uncle," so it was probably no big deal for Ella Marian, but for me… well, it was unexpectedly sweet.

When I glanced back at Tristan in time to see him wink at me, my heart felt warm and full. These people were incredibly kind and welcoming even though they hadn't known of my existence in the family tree until a year ago. Despite already having plenty of people to include in their family events, they hadn't hesitated to make room for me, too.

I cleared my throat. "I once worked the holiday season at the gift-wrapping kiosk in the mall. If anyone needs any help…"

Within moments, I was whisked away to the large sunroom by several eager takers until I was elbow-deep in wrapping paper, ribbon, scissors, and tape. The bright Colorado sun shone into the large windows and streaked across my worktable, and someone had put holiday music on the sound system. The tree lights flickered and the fire crackled while I demonstrated my special method of making bows. Sassy helped loop the ribbon, and Augie cut short lengths to tie the loops together with. We ended up making a kind of assembly line until the stack of beautifully wrapped gifts under the tree began to grow.

"You're handling everything very well," Augie said softly after a while.

"I'm good with my fingers. My mom begged me to take piano when I was younger," I admitted.

He chuckled softly. "No, I mean the family. The overwhelming Wilde-ness of this crew. It's… a lot."

I looked around the room at the Marians and Wildes who'd wandered in after breakfast and found somewhere to sit in the large, comfortable gathering space. Doc was grinning into his coffee mug while Grandpa whispered something in his ear.

47

Rebecca was gently pressing Thad on when he was going to stop traveling the world and settle down, preferably in the Bay Area. Griff was sprawled out on the floor stacking blocks for little Wolfe while his husband, Sam, scratched his back under an old wash-worn T-shirt that seemed to have said Made Marian at some point.

"They're good people," I said to Augie. "And I'm so grateful I found them... *you*... but I can't deny it takes some getting used to."

His giggle turned into a snort. Augie's laughter was contagious. After we both dissolved into a fit of laughter, Saint walked over to see what was so funny. He lifted his much-smaller husband off his chair, stole his seat, and then pulled Augie back down on his lap. "Something set you off. What was it?"

"Understatement," he stammered. "We're talking about your family."

Saint pressed a kiss into Augie's temple. "Pretty sure I have a piece of paper that makes them your family, too, sweetheart." He glanced away from Augie enough to smile at me. "But I get it. Sometimes being around these guys is more chaotic than being packed into a submarine like sardines."

"I didn't come from a big family either," Augie admitted. "And what I had of them wasn't at all welcoming. So it took me some time to get used to being around the Wildes."

"And then we found out about Grandpa's extended family, and shit got super nuts," Saint said. "Have we thanked you for that yet?"

Augie punched Saint on his broad shoulder and muttered an apology to me, but I knew he was just teasing. Anyone who cared about Grandpa and Tilly could see how grateful they were to be in one another's lives again.

"Where did Tilly and the ladies go?" I asked.

"Shopping," Felix said, moving over to nudge Saint and Augie out of the chair next to mine. "Beat it. I need professional help with this one, and Miller is my only hope."

He plunked down an oddly shaped wooden piece that looked

like either a fraternity spanking paddle or an old-fashioned game of some kind. I blinked up at him.

"Beg your pardon?"

Felix sighed. "Tabletop cornhole. You try buying something for a damned *king*. It's not as easy as one would think."

Saint snickered. "Lior is obsessed with Americana. Good choice, cuz."

Felix waved him away and slid the corn hole game at me. "Good luck and Godspeed. If you need to get out of any dodgy international kerfuffles, hit me up. I'll totes owe you one after this, and I have access to an intelligence agency."

As I began to tackle wrapping the challenging shape, Felix kept me company. He asked me about work, whether or not I'd heard that a book we both liked was being made into a movie, and how I was enjoying the Colorado mountain weather.

We'd met once before at the vineyard in Napa when the Wildes and Marians had gotten together, and I was pleasantly surprised to learn he'd remembered several of the things we'd talked about. When I finally put the bow on the wrapped gift and handed him a gift tag to fill out, he squeezed my hand.

"And how are you doing since losing your mom?" he asked in a gentle voice. "I was so sorry to hear about her passing. I know Grandpa was devastated, and I'm sure Tilly and Harold were, too. Kelly was a wonderful woman."

I glanced over at my own grandfather, Harold Cannon, who was sitting in an overstuffed armchair, reading a picture book to Pete and Ginger's son, Tommy. Harold must have sensed my gaze because he looked up and met my eye. His face brightened, and I couldn't help but smile at him. Here was yet another example of someone who should have seemed larger-than-life to me—his reputation as a senator and the father of a US president was intimidating as hell—but was incredibly kind and loving, welcoming and accepting.

And he'd been my mother's biological father. Only... she'd never known him until shortly before her death. The injustice of it galled me. She hadn't had enough time with them. I almost felt guilty for being here with her big extensive family when she herself had never had the chance to spend this much time with them.

But then I thought about Darius saying this extended family was an amazing gift my mother had given me before leaving, and I felt the truth of it down to my bones.

I swallowed past a lump in my throat. "Thank you. I'm doing okay. We had the chance to say our goodbyes, and I know she was beyond ready to go. That has made it easier. Wishing she was still here feels selfish because I know she was in pain."

Felix nodded. "Do you have other friends to support you back home?"

I thought about my good friends in Monterey. I'd only lived there for a few years, but I'd made some lifelong friends in that short time. "Yes, I have several neighbors who have been incredible, and I play Ultimate Frisbee with a great group of guys who've been there for me through all of this. Tilly and Harold came down and stayed with us for those final few months, and Granny and Irene came down a few times, too. Rebecca calls me every week and mails me homemade meals, if you can believe it."

He chuckled. "I remember when she met West for the first time. She came to see Nico and help him with Pippa. As soon as she realized Nico and West were a couple, she started sending him cookies in the mail. Only, since he's a doctor, she made sure they were healthy. Like, avocado instead of butter and stuff like that. Ugh."

Felix couldn't see, but Rebecca was standing just behind him. "I heard that, Felix Grimaldi. Ask West who his favorite cookie-maker is. I dare you."

Felix opened his mouth—presumably to apologize—but West beat him to the punch. "Definitely Nico. You can't be married to a bakery owner and answer any other way, Rebecca. Sorry, ma'am."

I'd forgotten about Nico's bakery. Sugar Britches was a small bakery in Hobie, Texas, located underneath Nico's famous tattoo shop. Since the man was known for his ink, it was easy to forget about the bakery. I wondered if Darius and Nico would enjoy connecting to talk about their common businesses.

Nico walked up to Rebecca and put his arm around her shoulders. "Ignore him. He's trying to suck up to me because he made me get up with Reenie in the middle of the night last night even though it was his turn. We all know I don't do any of the baking. Stevie and his crew do all the work at Sugar Britches."

Rebecca sighed. "I wish Stevie and Evan had been able to come."

Nico laughed. "There's not enough room in Aster Valley for that man's personality. Besides, he hates the cold. And he loves the holiday season at the bakery. His sister is in a production of the Nutcracker they're doing at her dance school. You couldn't have dragged him away from that either."

West muttered a good-natured "Thank god" before handing me another awkward gift to wrap. "It's a dildo in the shape of a boat anchor," he whispered. "Worth wanted me to ask you to wrap it for Cal. After I punched him in the face for defiling my baby brother, I agreed. But only after I also got him to promise me a week on the yacht with Nico for our five-year anniversary. I figure it'll be that long before we can comfortably farm out the girls to someone else."

I stared at him before blushing as red as an apple at Rebecca. She sighed. "If you think I'm not immune to sex toy talk by now, you're shockingly misinformed. And West? I'm happy to come to Hobie anytime to watch the girls and visit with Doc and Grandpa. Maybe plan it for your three-year celebration instead," she suggested before leaving the room in search of a fresh cup of coffee.

Nico smiled after her. "That woman is a saint."

"What?" Saint called from where he'd moved Augie to a snuggle by the fireplace.

"Not you, asshole," West called back. "A real saint."

"Anyway," Felix said, grumbling at his cousin. "As I was getting ready to say, if you find yourself in need of a vacation — either from this madness," he said, gesturing to the room at large, "or from Monterey and memories of your mom, we'd love to host you at our place anytime."

Lior, who'd come into the room quietly and sat on the floor

by Felix's feet a few minutes before, lifted his head from Felix's lap. "I agree. We'd love to have you, and I can promise no Wildes or Marians in the entire place." He shot a look at his husband and stifled a grin. "Anymore."

Max Wilde huffed. "Remember what I said about being a peasant? This is exactly what I mean. You royals have no respect for the servant class. I live in the palace with you." He tacked on a sarcastic "Your Majesty" at the end.

Lior didn't even turn his head, but he did roll his eyes and raise his patrician countenance. "Ignore him. Plebes don't count. Clearly."

Arthur sniffed loudly. "Note to self: special-order itching powder and accidentally dust it over the royal bedding."

"Hey!" Felix said. "I don't deserve that. I don't treat Max like a peasant. More like a pesky baby brother."

Lior sighed. "I don't think you can call it royal bedding if it comes from Bed Bath & Beyond."

The horrified look on Arthur's face set me off. I started laughing, which made Felix and Max both laugh, too.

"I beg your pardon," Arthur said, clutching at his throat. "I'll have you know those sheets were made from the cocoons of Mulberry silkworms."

"Gross," Felix said. "Why can't we have the ones from Bed Bath & Beyond? Those probably kill less animals during manufacturing."

Arthur took a calming breath. "I assure you, all of the royal silk is procured from sources that utilize the Ahimsa method of waiting for the silkworm to escape before removing the cocoon. And if you think you'd be doing the world a service by selecting cotton instead, you obviously remain uninformed that cotton is the most heavily sprayed crop there is. High water use and the use of harmful pesticides and insecticides contribute to…"

I stopped listening as he droned on about cotton production. Rebecca had entered the room looking like the bearer of bad news.

"Harold," she said, making her way toward my grandfather.

"Mikey has just been contacted by the Aster Valley sheriff. It seems Tilly and the others have been arrested."

Harold sighed in a resigned sort of way. "Again? What for this time?"

Even though I'd heard stories about Tilly, Granny, and Irene getting into trouble in the past, this was the first time I'd been around for it. Unlike everyone else in the room, I panicked. Tilly was in her eighties. As feisty as she might have been, she wouldn't fare well in jail, even for a short time.

Rebecca handed me the now-familiar keys to Mikey's SUV. "According to the sheriff, they're unsure which charges will stick. But the choices are the usual. Public indecency, public nuisance, theft, vandalism, and abduction. Mikey suggests the abduction charge is a stretch."

Harold stood up and patted his back pocket to make sure he had his wallet. "Who the hell did she abduct?"

"One of the sleigh ride horses at the Christmas tree farm."

Harold and I blinked at her for a split second before the room erupted in laughter and strong opinions. I couldn't believe they'd be so unfeeling as to laugh at a time like this. What if she was hurt? Was it possible a woman like Tilly would know how to handle a giant draft horse? What if she was cold? It was freezing outside, and she barely had any body fat.

Rebecca patted the keys in my hand. "Go. I'll hold them off as long as I can. Lord only knows how Aster Valley would handle a love posse."

I'd heard her use that phrase before, but I'd never been quite sure what it meant. After only being here for a little while, I was beginning to understand.

6

DARIUS

I was walking out of the county clerk's office when I happened to
see Miller Hobbs racing into the sheriff's office next door with a
clear look of fear on his face. An attractive, somewhat familiar
older man with white hair held on to his elbow as they pushed
through the glass doors.

Without thinking, I turned on my heel and followed them. As
soon as I got inside, I heard Miller pleading with the
receptionist.

"My grandmother has been detained, and I need to see her."

"Name."

"Miller Hobbs," he said in a rush.

The receptionist's lip twitched. "Name of incarcerated."

Miller groaned as if in pain. "She'd better not be incarcerated. She didn't do anything wrong... or, well, she didn't mean
anything by it if she did."

The receptionist shook her head and sighed. "They
never do."

The man with the white hair stepped forward. "My name is
Harold Cannon. Matilda Marian is my wife."

As soon as I heard him give his name, I realized why he
looked familiar. Senator Cannon, father of *President* Cannon, was

political royalty. What was Miller doing here with him in the Rockley County Sheriff's Office?

"Miller?" I said softly. Miller turned around and spotted me by the doors, but before he could say anything, the receptionist told Senator Cannon he could go back and see his wife.

The senator murmured a few words to Miller before leaving him alone in the lobby to disappear behind a locked door. Miller turned back to me and twisted his hands together in front of him as if trying to keep them from doing something else. "What are you doing here?"

"I saw you out on the street and wanted to find out if you needed any help."

"I... I don't know. It's my grandmother. She and her friends were arrested. We came to find out what's going on."

The door to the street opened behind me, blowing in frigid air from outside. I quickly moved closer to Miller just as a crowd of people came in. Everyone was talking at once, and the noise level skyrocketed.

Within seconds, I was jostled to the side as several men approached Miller. One pulled him into a tight embrace. "How are you holding up? Any news?"

Even though I had no right to feel this way, I was annoyed at the man's familiarity with Miller. Everyone swarmed around him, and it didn't take me long to determine this was the lovably chaotic family he'd mentioned to me. I let out a breath and started to move back toward the door to leave them in peace. Clearly, he'd have all the help he needed. Senator Cannon would have unlimited resources with any law enforcement agency, and there had to be an attorney or two among the large group surrounding Miller.

"Wait," Miller blurted, grasping my hand and holding it tight. "Don't leave. I mean... unless you need to. I'd really like you to stay. If you don't mind."

I stepped closer again and squeezed his hand. My heartbeat ticked up. "Of course I don't mind. I'll stay as long as you need me."

As soon as the people around Miller realized he was holding

a stranger's hand, they began to demand an introduction. I met more people than I could ever recall names for, but a few notable ones stood out. One of his cousins was a famous country music singer, more attractive in person than I'd ever seen him on television or the internet. Another was an actual royal consort, which had to be some kind of joke. I'd put Google to the test later to see if I was being pranked. And then there was a man with long red hair who spoke in a lovely Irish accent and whose husband looked at him like he was the second coming of Christ.

For that matter, many of the men looked at their spouses that way in this group, and it only took a few moments to determine the rumor was true. Mikey and Tiller were hosting a large collection of beautiful gay men at the lodge this week. I just hadn't realized they were almost all already taken.

That was fine by me. As long as Miller wasn't taken, I was happy.

"She's probably being strip-searched," someone said. Someone else mumbled something about her most likely enjoying it.

I felt Miller tense beside me.

"Knowing Granny, she's probably already trading sexual favors for a better bed," someone else suggested with a laugh.

"Or she's giving lessons," another guy added.

As they continued to joke around, Miller got more and more restless until I offered to walk him outside for a breath of fresh air.

"No, I... I want to ask for an update. Why is this taking so long?"

Another older gentleman I hadn't noticed before made his way through the throng to pull Miller into a hug. "She'll be okay. You know how much she loves a good story, and this will inevitably turn into one of her favorites."

"Why does she always have to do stuff like this?" Miller said into the man's shoulder. "I worry about her. What if..."

The gentleman pulled away and held Miller by the shoulders. "There's not a chance in hell they'll keep her locked up for hijacking a sleigh ride. At most, they'll charge her a fine

56

and give her a warning. She'll likely make a large donation to the sleigh owner regardless, and that'll be that. Not many people begrudge little old ladies a moment of temporary insanity."

Miller nodded and realized it was time for more introductions. "Grandpa, this is Darius Grant. Darius, this is Wes Wilde, my great-uncle. And everyone else here is pretty much a second cousin."

I shook the man's hand. "Nice to meet you, sir."

Anyone around us who hadn't already seen me began to take notice there was a stranger in their midst. Several raised eyebrows and quirky grins warned me that a boatload of teasing was incoming.

"Well, well, well," a woman with a big mane of dark curly hair said, making her way over to us. "And who might you be?"

Miller blushed. "Simone, this is Darius. He's the man who made the baklava you cried over last night."

Simone's grin dropped, and she clapped a hand over her heart. "You made that? I want to marry that baklava. Holy cow. Tell me everything. How do you make it? Where do I get the recipe? I've never had baklava like that."

A large, muscled guy stepped up and reached out a hand to shake. "I'm Simone's husband, Joel. Nice to meet you. Please forgive my wife. She's in the cravings stage of pregnancy."

She glared at him. "I'm not pregnant, asshole."

We all looked down at her obvious bump.

"Fine," she said, throwing up her arms. "I'm pregnant. I was going to surprise everyone on Christmas Day. There, are you happy now?"

Joel wrapped his arm around her and smiled wide. "Super happy. Also? You told everyone last night you needed a fourth piece of baklava 'for the baby,' so I kinda assumed you'd already spilled the beans."

"Wasn't she just pregnant like two months ago?" someone else asked.

"She's always pregnant," someone else replied.

I had to admit, I kind of liked this family already. But I could tell Miller was getting more and more uncomfortable the longer we went without an update about his grandmother.

"Do you want me to ask them what's going on?" I murmured into his ear. "I know Sheriff Stone. I can ask if he's here."

Miller shot me a grateful look and nodded. "If you don't mind."

I left him with his cousins and made my way to the reception counter. "Is Declan here?"

The receptionist nodded. "Yes, but he's dealing with a situation at the moment," she said, tilting her head toward the crowd in the lobby.

"I was hoping to get an update on that situation. What if I promised him a dozen bear claws if he can tell us what's going on?"

Her face cracked into a wide grin. "You sure know the way to our sheriff's heart, don't you? You must be the new baker they all keep talking about. My aunt Peg says your sugar cookies are to die for."

After sweet-talking her a little longer, the receptionist finally agreed to go find out what was taking so long. Within moments, the locked door to the back opened, letting Senator Cannon out with a lovely older woman on his arm and two more ladies trailing behind. The tiniest one was spewing profanities.

"Not a single damned strip search. What's the world coming to when a woman can't even get a little action in the pokey?"

The tall woman sighed. "I offered you action, and you declined."

The little one flapped her hand in the air. "I can get that action any old time."

The tall one lifted an imperious eyebrow. "Can you?"

Miller surprised everyone by racing to his grandmother and throwing his arms around her. I could tell she was one of the most surprised, but then she quickly squeezed her eyes closed and tightened her arms around him. "I'm okay, child. No harm done," she seemed to say before pulling back and offering him a reassuring smile. I moved a little closer so I could hear better. "It was a lot of stuff and nonsense over a simple sleigh ride."

Senator Cannon added, "A simple sleigh ride in which the three of you hijacked the sleigh, lifted your shirts to flash a large man in a snowman costume, and caused a stampede."

Miller's grandmother patted her hair into place. "We were under the mistaken impression they had beads to throw," she said with a sniff. "Never trust a six-and-a-half-foot snow beast to know what's what."

"Are you okay, though?" Miller demanded. "I was worried you might have gotten hurt."

"Nothing a hot toddy and a long nap won't cure, I'm sure," she said with a wave of her hand before catching sight of me. "And who might this young stud be?"

I stepped forward and noticed Miller's cheeks turn a light shade of pink. "Tilly, this is Darius Grant. He's the owner of Honey's, the bakery that's been providing the sweets at the lodge."

Tilly looked me up and down. "I see."

I resisted the urge to fidget. "It's nice to meet you, Tilly," I said. "I'm happy to see you on this side of the door."

"Thank you. And what exactly are your intentions with my grandson?"

I blinked at her while Miller sputtered and tried to erase her question from the ether. "Tilly! That's... he's... it's none of your business."

I placed my hand on his lower back. "I intend to get to know him better," I said firmly. "In our own time. And hopefully discover that you're the only dangerous criminal in his family."

Her eyes locked on mine for a long beat of silence before she broke out in laughter. "Oh, honey. I like you. But I'm naught but a lowly horse thief. Hardly a dangerous criminal."

I nodded with a grin. "I believe they stopped hanging horse thieves in the 1800s, so you're probably right."

Miller made a strangled sound in his throat. "Hanging? Can we please get out of here? Are you free to go?"

Senator Cannon reached out to shake my hand. Miller performed another quick introduction before Tilly interjected. "Darius, dear, might I have a private word before we leave?"

I wondered if this was when I would get the kind of dressing-down I'd heard about in novels and old movies, a kind of warning against treating her grandson with disrespect.

"Certainly," I said, gesturing her off to the side. Miller shot me a nervous glance, but I responded with what I hoped was a reassuring smile.

When we were out of earshot, she lost her easy smile and suddenly looked much older. "Is there any way you can take him away from this crowd for a few hours? I can tell he was truly worried, and it can only be exacerbated by the poor sleep he's been getting. I regret causing him concern, and I may have over-looked the fact he's not as familiar with my antics as the others." She looked momentarily regretful, and I imagined that was unusual for her. "I'm afraid if he returns with us to the lodge, he'll fuss over me like a mother hen. I'd much rather him be distracted in… some way."

I studied her. It felt an awful lot like she was asking me to distract him with my…

"What are you talking about over here?" Simone butted into our private conversation before my imagination got away from me. "Tilly, stop harassing poor Darius. This isn't like Christmas two years ago when we set Noah up with all those blind dates."

Tilly tapped her chin with a red-tipped fingernail. "No… but it could be." She narrowed her eyes at me. "Should we set Miller up on several dates this holiday season, Darius?"

"Yes, ma'am," I said, enjoying the surprised disappointment on her face. "Only make sure they're all with me."

Simone and Tilly both laughed and let me return to Miller's side.

"Can I give you a ride home?" I offered in a low voice.

Miller bit his lip. "Oh, I can probably catch a ride back with everyone else."

"I was hoping you'd let me swing by my place first and pick up some extra baklava for Simone." It wasn't exactly a lie. I would be sure to send him home with baklava later.

He relaxed and smiled sweetly. "Of course. That's so nice of you."

I led him outside to my truck and handed him in before moving around to the driver's side. We rode the first few minutes in silence before Miller realized we weren't headed to the bakery. "I thought Honey's is that way," he said, pointing out the window.

"The baklava is at my house. Do you mind?"

He blew out a breath. "No, actually. That's better. I've had enough of people today." He seemed to second-guess his statement. "Not that I don't love it at Honey's! And Hannah is super nice. I'm sorry."

I reached over and squeezed his hand. "I understand what you're trying to say. You'd prefer some peace and quiet. That was partly why I offered to drive you."

Miller turned to me. "You must think I'm odd."

I turned the truck up the mountain road. "Not even a little bit." Extraordinary, unique, *precious*. Those were the words I'd use to describe Miller Hobbs. But I didn't want to frighten him off by saying so.

"One of the reasons I took the job for Happy Teeth is because it allowed me to work from home. I moved in with my mom to help take care of her, and I was able to balance that with work pretty easily. Unfortunately, it meant I got out of the habit of being around a lot of people. It's a little hard getting used to it again."

I shrugged. "That makes sense, and you don't have to explain yourself to me. Not everyone is energized by a crowd."

"What about you?"

I took a minute to think about my answer before speaking. "I like being around people, but I have a tendency to get competitive and overwork when I'm in a fast-paced environment. You remember me telling you I moved here because I didn't like who I was back in Chicago?"

He nodded.

"I want a more peaceful lifestyle. I'd like a chance for my customers to become my friends. I want to have days like this where I can actually leave when the baking is done and spend time with someone I..." I cleared my throat. "Like."

61

Miller's shy smile was worth the awkwardness I felt.

"I'd like that... that kind of lifestyle too," Miller admitted. "I've thought about opening my own marketing consulting company and pitching marketing services to local businesses in Monterey. Creating websites, enabling online ordering for shops like yours, proposing multimedia campaigns that pair the right kind of marketing with their product lines, and maybe even dabbling in some branding and graphic design consulting."

I didn't want to blurt out the suggestion of him doing all of that here in Aster Valley, but it was hard to keep the thought to myself. "You could always rent one of those shared workspaces so you weren't so isolated," I suggested.

We continued to talk through ideas until I pulled into my driveway. Miller's voice trailed off when he noticed my house.

"Is this yours?" he asked in awe.

I looked at the mountainside property with pride. The glass-and-steel structure didn't leave much in the way of privacy, but since it was situated in the middle of eighteen acres, the neighbors were hidden behind plenty of trees.

"I originally had it built as a vacation home but then fell in love with it and decided to move here full-time."

"It's incredible. The views... Can I see inside?"

I wanted to laugh with abandon. Miller Hobbs was inviting himself into my house? Yes, please. "Of course. Come on in and let's get you warmed up."

After opening the door and ushering him into the main living area that was a large open space with expansive views of Aster Valley and the entire Rockley basin, Miller did what everyone did when they first came inside. He walked straight to the wall of windows and stood gaping. "Just the other day I was wondering what the view looked like from these houses. It's even more stunning than I expected. No wonder you decided to move here."

I came up behind him and reached for his coat, peeling it back before grabbing the warm hat off his head. "Have a seat. That sofa there has the best view, and it's close to the fireplace."

After hanging our coats up, I lit the fire and stayed long

enough to make sure it was going to turn into a sufficient blaze to keep him toasty. "How about some hot chocolate or tea?"

"I'd love some hot chocolate if you have it. Can I help in the kitchen?"

"Not necessary. I'll have it ready in a minute. Just relax."

I turned on some soft instrumental music on the house sound system and busied myself with making us a tray of drinks and snacks. When I brought it over to him, I noticed his eyelids drooping. He'd curled up in the corner of the sofa and pulled a blanket over his legs. I loved seeing that he'd made himself comfortable in my home without me having to say anything. It had to be a testament to how easy and relaxed he felt in my presence.

I kept the conversation to a minimum as we ate and drank so as to let him nod off after we finished. Sure enough, his eyes drooped while he was still holding his mug, and I had to lunge forward to keep it from spilling onto the rug.

For the next two hours, I was able to look my fill of his beautiful face and revel in the knowledge he was safe and sound, here with me. In an effort to avoid the temptation of snuggling him without his consent, I busied myself in the kitchen, where I could keep an eye on him across the open floor plan while I made the baklava I'd promised him.

I made enough to feed an army since that was exactly what Mikey and Tiller had over there. When I packaged it up, I made sure to put a good amount into its own box just for Simone. When I finished the baklava, I started on avgolemono soup with some leftover rotisserie chicken and homemade chicken stock I had in the freezer. Even though I knew Mikey would provide more than enough food for everyone over at the lodge, I still needed to send Miller home with something I'd made especially for him.

It was a family thing. My yaya had never let a guest leave with empty hands, and I found myself doing the same as I got older. Food was my family's expression of love.

When Miller finally started waking up, I moved back over to the sofa and knelt on the floor next to him. His face was pink and smooth from sleeping close to the fire, and a rogue blonde wave went the wrong way on the side of his head that had been pressed against a throw pillow. I reached out to smooth it down.

"Feel any better?" I asked with a teasing grin.

For a split second, he looked horrified as the realization he'd fallen asleep on me crashed through him. But then a moment later, he huffed out a smile. "I guess I made myself right at home."

"I guess you did."

I kept running my fingers through his hair as if all the thick blond strands needed smoothing. They didn't.

Our eyes met and stayed locked together for a heavy beat before Miller blinked and looked away self-consciously. "How long did I sleep?"

I moved my hand to his cheek and gently turned his face back toward me. "Just long enough."

His eyebrows furrowed in confusion, and I could no longer resist leaning in to press a lingering kiss against his warm cheek.

Miller's breath hitched, and his hand came out instinctively to clutch the fabric of my shirt over my chest. He turned his head toward me until our lips brushed together. It was featherlight at first, teasing and barely there. But then we fell into a wordless duel. Our mouths flirted with each other, feinting and parrying, until both of us had silly grins on our faces.

I finally couldn't take it anymore and tackled him on the sofa, pushing him down and devouring his lush mouth until both of us were rock hard and panting. Miller's hard cock arched up against mine, and his hands grabbed my ass possessively.

Gone was the unsure man from the bakery, and in his place was a passionate, engaged, confident lover.

"Want you," Miller gasped between kisses. "Please."

I nipped at the side of his neck and reached down to rub his dick through his pants at the same time. "Want you, too."

My head was filled with visions of Miller naked and begging, spread out on the rug in front of the fireplace. I imagined his hole slick and soft after long, edging prep. My tongue could almost taste the hard peaks of his nipples and smell the masculine scent of his body as I nosed my way down to suck him off.

The shrill peal of my phone alarm interrupted our foreplay, and it took me several long moments of confusion before I could place what that meant.

I dropped several softer kisses on his neck, jaw, and cheek before climbing off him. "It's late. That's my reminder alarm. I'm teaching a class tonight and need to get to the bakery to gather everything I need. Sorry, I didn't realize how late it had gotten."

Miller sat up and straightened his clothes. "Shit. Sorry. I didn't know…"

"Of course not. I think it's a surprise."

Miller's face crinkled into confusion again. "What do you mean?"

I reached out a hand to pull him off the sofa. "My class tonight is at Rockley Lodge. I'm teaching a beautiful, sexy man and his family how to decorate holiday cookies."

Miller's jaw dropped in surprise, and I took the opportunity to steal another kiss before hustling him out the door.

7

MILLER

I was feeling an odd combination of excitement and nerves. Darius was going to spend the evening with my entire family? Since when? And why hadn't he mentioned it before now?

After dropping me off at the lodge, he left to do his prep work at the bakery. I took the stack of baklava boxes and the bag with the chicken soup into the kitchen, where Tiller and Mikey were having a quiet conversation in front of the large commercial range.

They stood close together with Tiller's large hand spread across Mikey's lower back. Tiller held Mikey to him while he spoke to him with a soft, affectionate smile. As soon as they heard the crinkle of the paper bag I carried, they turned and greeted me.

"There you are," Mikey said. "You were gone all day. Did you have a nice time with Darius?"

I set my spoils on the kitchen island. "I fell asleep on him," I admitted. "He lit a fire and put on some music... next thing I knew, I was drooling all over myself."

Tiller laughed and stepped closer to help unpack the goodies. "Mikey's been known to drool in Darius's presence also. It's not uncommon."

Mikey made a disgruntled sound and swatted at Tiller's ass. "I drool over the bakery treats, not the baker himself."

Tiller shot me a knowing look. "We'll allow him his denials as long as he allows us to drool too. Darius is a fine-looking man, isn't he?"

I opened my mouth to respond, but I mostly sputtered out something incomprehensible like, "M'hmpf, nut puticular norflup." I'd meant to say something suave like, "Hm, not that I noticed in particular," but it came out at the same time as, "Mm-hm, yup," and got kind of mixed together. Tiller and Mikey howled with laughter.

"Gurl, same," Mikey said between giggles.

I sighed. "Anyone have a fire extinguisher I can use on my face real quick? Thanks."

Tiller pulled out a triangle of baklava and handed it to me. "Here, busy yourself with this. You'll forget all about how beautiful that Greek man is."

But he was so wrong, and he knew it. One bite of the honey-rich pastry sent images of Darius screaming through my mind. "Fucking Christ," I muttered around the flaky bite. It was one of the best things I'd ever tasted, and it had been made with tender care, specifically for my family.

Blue Marian walked into the kitchen and asked what I was moaning over. "Try this," I said, reaching for a triangle to share with him. "Baklava from the bakery in town."

As more and more people heard the commotion in the kitchen, the space quickly filled with grandparents, great-uncles, cousins, kids, and everyone else who was here with our group. Someone put on holiday music, and someone else offered to help Mikey with the final efforts involved in getting dinner on the table for such a large crew.

When we finally sat down in the largest dining room, Thomas Marian stood up to make a toast.

"Rebecca, don't look at me, or I'll get emotional," he warned without looking at his wife. The statement alone made me emotional. Rebecca and Thomas were a true example of long-term love and commitment.

He cleared his throat and continued. "I know it's not Christmas yet, but this is as good a time as any to give thanks and celebrate. How fortunate we are to have such an incredible group of family and friends gathered together. Thank you all for making the effort to get here. I know it's not easy to get time off from work, leave your pets and calendars behind, and prioritize a reunion trip like this, but it's important. Family is important."

Everyone smiled warmly and glanced around the room to take in the sea of faces as Thomas continued.

"When Aunt Tilly suggested this trip as a way to get the Wilde and Marian sides of the family together, I knew it would be special. But I didn't anticipate how special it would be to see Aunt Tilly together with Uncle Wes... Grandpa to most of you... and it makes me wish..." He took a moment to clear his throat again. "I know in my heart my father is looking down on his brother and sister and the many beautiful lives the three of you have created, and he's in awe the way I am. What an incredible testament to the strength and power of family. But that's not all."

Simone spoke under her breath like an infomercial announcer, "But wait, there's more!" And everyone chuckled and wiped a few stray tears.

"Yes, daughter," he said, reaching over and squeezing her shoulder. "There is more. All of you who've joined us by choice. Those of you who met one of us and gifted us with your love. There is more to family than blood, of course. There is the family of our hearts. And regardless of how you came to be here tonight, I want you to know I love you all so much, and I feel humbled by your choice to be here, to be a part of this family, and to continue to love us all."

He finally turned toward Rebecca, who was smiling through some tears. "I especially thank you for being here," he said in a voice quickly overtaken with a rough croaking sound. "Thank you for loving me. For giving me six beautiful children and helping us welcome and love four more and then their ten partners. I am overwhelmed with gratitude."

The entire room dissolved into a bawling mess.

And that's when Darius walked in.

The look on his face was comical. It was clear he misinterpreted the heavy emotion. He raced over to me and pulled my chair back until I faced him. He searched my face frantically. "Dear god. What happened?"

I stood without thinking and leaned into his embrace as his arms came tightly around me. "It's fine. Everything is fine, I promise." Feeling his arms around me and seeing the concern on his face when he thought I might be upset was everything. It almost made me feel like I had one of the spouses Thomas had mentioned in his toast.

"Hear, hear," someone yelled, and everyone cheered and took a sip of whatever they were drinking.

Mikey quickly found a chair to squeeze in next to me, and Darius joined us for dinner. It was as loud and raucous as one might imagine, but Darius seemed to handle it without a problem. He talked animatedly to Otto on the other side of him and Ginger across the table.

At one point, Tilly caught my eye and gave me a wink. Her smile was relaxed, and she seemed completely at peace. She must have slept the afternoon away the same way I had. I was relieved to see her so at ease after her ordeal.

Dinner passed quickly, and several people offered to help Mikey and Tiller clean up in the kitchen so Darius could use the space to teach us our cookie lesson. In the meantime, the rest of us bundled the younger kids up and took them outside to play in the snow that had begun to come down while we'd been at the table.

The California and Texas kids were thrilled at the novelty of it, and they wound up playing so hard they were ready for bed by the time Darius had everything set up in the clean kitchen.

The central island was enormous, but there was also room at the giant heavy wood table by the windows. The people interested in the cookie decorating lesson gathered around to hear Darius's instructions.

"Why are we doing this without the kids?" Tristan asked after Darius finished his explanations and allowed us to start decorating our own cookies. "Not that I mind, but I would have thought—"

"Because of cookie dick," Granny said absently.

Silence filled the room.

"Don't ask," Blue said quickly.

Unfortunately, it wasn't quick enough. At the same time, Ammon Marian, who was the youngest of my Marian cousins at just twenty years old, asked, "What's cookie dick?"

Charlie stepped forward and spoke with a serious expression. "You see, Ammon... when a boy indulges in too many cookies, sometimes he can't quite—"

Hudson clapped a hand over his mouth and yanked him back.

Otto made an exaggerated frown. "I thought that only happened with rum cake."

Seth shook his head. "You've obviously forgotten my mom's Bourbon Balls."

Otto opened his mouth—presumably to make a snarky comment about Seth's mom's balls—when Seth shot him a glare. Otto closed his mouth.

Teddy nodded. "My friend Mac makes eggnog thumbprints that'll put you on your ass. Cookie dick is no joke."

King glanced at Falcon. "I thought it only happened with those Hungarian pálinka things. You know, the chocolate cherry ones we had that night you decided to—"

Now it was Falcon's turn to muzzle his husband. "Bup, bup, bup. No need to bring that up. Everyone would prefer if it stayed buried in the past. For a sneaky cat burglar, you're surprisingly terrible at keeping secrets."

Tilly narrowed her eyes at them with suspicion. "I wouldn't prefer it. In fact, I'd like to know about it. What happened that night with the chocolate cherry booze bombs?"

Falcon's cheeks turned red. "Cookie dick. Apparently."

"Thankfully, it didn't affect his mouth," King said proudly. Falcon smacked him on the chest.

I noticed Darius chuckling to himself before he glanced up and shot me a wink. "You okay?" he mouthed.

"Embarrassed," I mouthed back.

He winked at me, making my stomach tighten with need. He was so damned sexy standing there among my family with his capable, easy manner. Everyone seemed to take to him right away. He smiled and explained things like he'd taught this class a million times and still loved doing it.

I'd had the benefit of seeing Darius decorate the cookies earlier with a colorful string of lights, so I copied his idea and made several variations of his design. Felix sat quietly beside me with a large circular cookie he was painting into a masterful swirling design bursting with bright color.

"It's the Glory Window from the Chapel of Thanksgiving in Dallas," he murmured, without taking his eyes off the detail work. "It gets brighter as it spirals up."

"That's gorgeous," I said. "I've never heard of it, but it looks like a place worth visiting."

"Mm, if you like this, there's a mosque in Iran that uses the same sort of light and color technique."

I glanced over at his husband's masterpiece, which was a Santa shape he'd frosted to look like Angela Merkel. Lior met my eyes and answered the question I hadn't dared ask. "She's oddly compelling in person. Also, if you Instagram her likeness, she sends you a bottle of Himbeergeist, which is a raspberry liquor that tastes amazing over ice cream."

Arthur piped up from the tidy Christmas wreath he was frosting. "She only does that for you, sir. And I'm fairly certain the symbolism goes over your head."

Lior frowned. "What symbolism?"

Felix spoke without looking up. "She's giving you a raspberry."

Lior looked confused. "Not an actual —"

Max made an indelicate fart sound with his mouth. "Raspberry," he said.

Lior's mouth opened in surprise. "That Miststück," he said in dawning comprehension. "How dare she?"

Felix reached out blindly and patted his husband's arm. "I already sent her a bird, dear. It's fine."

71

Lior blinked. "Tell me you didn't."

Arthur somehow managed to retain his dignity as he nodded. "Indeed he did, sir. It was a beautiful fascinator made on an oval pillbox hat with a bird sporting an extravagant selection of feathers. It's a fascinator fit for a queen, if I may say so. Your king consort has quite a refined sense of taste."

Lior's eyes squeezed closed. "This is how wars begin."

I started giggling and couldn't stop. Darius came over to ask what had set me off, and I gasped through my attempt at explaining. Once I'd started laughing, Felix had, too, and soon Max joined in. Before long, half the kitchen was in hysterics.

And then Granny held up her cookie dick.

Darius stared at the monstrosity. Somehow, Granny had managed to use frosting to glue two wreath cookies to the bottom of a candy cane cookie. She iced the entire thing in a horrid light pink she must have made with red and white, and then she sprinkled brown jimmies onto the wreaths and added marshmallow creme to the tip.

And that wasn't the worst of it.

"I made a hole," Irene said proudly, holding up a matching flesh-colored wreath cookie with chocolate jimmies sprinkled a little too liberally around the hole. "And the cookie dick fits in it perfectly."

Granny's eyes twinkled. "Slides right in like a treat."

"Ouch," someone muttered.

Darius opened his mouth to speak but paused for a moment as if gathering his thoughts. "Great. Great job, ladies. If only I'd known you'd want to make... adult-themed shapes, I could have whipped out some of my special cookie cutters for the occasion."

"He said whipped," someone snickered.

Dante Marian shook his head. "They're like little boys playing with guns. You don't have to give them actual dicks for them to make dicks with whatever they can find on hand."

Now it was Tilly who snickered. "Dicks on hand."

"I beg your pardon," Granny said. "I made a feminine power bundle before I ventured into male genitalia."

I grabbed Darius's arm. "Don't ask. I beg you."

72

Granny didn't wait to be asked anyway. "That's the whole kit and caboodle. Vag, clit... well, here. Take a look."

When she pulled another cookie from her plate, I gasped and looked away before getting up the nerve to peek again.

Darius's sexy voice murmured in my ear. "Is that..."

I didn't dare respond, but Jude made an affirmative noise. "Mmhm. Looks like the ball on top of Santa's hat has been put to good use."

MJ Wilde looked on appreciatively. "I'll say. That's one happy... hat. And are those..."

"All I had for the love flaps were these angel wings," Granny explained. "But you gotta admit it's downright appropriate."

I blocked out the rest of her soliloquy on "the effervescence of lady spirits" and tried desperately to focus on painting my simple snowman. But at that point, all I could see was a bumpy butt plug shape, and the entire process had lost a little of its magic.

"Lior, you should post *these* on Instagram!" Granny suggested.

"And get dethroned," Arthur said under his breath.

"No, thank you," Lior said politely while perfecting Angela Merkel's expression of dignified competence.

While helping clean up some of the trash around the counter and table, Tiller Raine asked Darius if Honey's had an Instagram account. "Not for those, obviously," he said, indicating the naughty cookies, "But for the rest of these and the class itself. Might be good PR if you want to book more cookie nights. The Riggers have a social media manager who was telling me just how influential the team's Instagram account has become."

Darius shook his head. "I haven't had time to start much social media besides our website."

Nico joined in. "Miller could help you start one. He manages the one for my tattoo shop now, and it's been incredible. We had one before but just threw pics up there randomly when we remembered. Miller does like hashtags and special features and all kinds of shit. Plus, he showed us how to take better pictures in the first place. We're getting inquiries from all over the country now, and our customers tag us in their own pics, too. He's going to show us how to do TikTok next."

I tried to focus on cleaning up my supplies, but I couldn't help listening for Darius's reply. "Really? I'd love to see the account. I'm a sucker for good ink, but maybe I can pick up some tips about posting, too."

He sounded impressed, which made my gut clench pleasantly.

"Yeah, sure, but I'm telling you. Get Miller to hook you up. He'll put linkie-things in your..." Nico looked down at my snowman butt plug cookie and cleared his throat. "Profile. And... what is that?"

"Snowman," I said at the same time Felix said, "Ziggy anal plug," without looking up from his stained glass masterpiece. "It's made out of borosilicate glass and features three graduated bulb... never mind."

I dropped my face in my hands. Darius's deep, warm laugh washed over me as he snuck his arms around me from behind. His lips brushed the back of my neck, and I shuddered.

"Come home with me tonight," he said softly enough that only I could hear him.

"You're asking me to leave all this behind?" I asked with a hint of sarcasm. His laugh rumbled through my back.

"Only temporarily. All this naughty talk is getting my candy cane... nope. I can't come up with anything nearly as funny as your family."

"Don't try," I said with a laugh. "I beg you."

His lips moved closer to my ear, and his voice dropped even lower. "You beg me? Mm. Hold that thought..."

Instead of feeling self-conscious, I relaxed against him before turning my head and pressing a kiss to his cheek and inhaling his unique scent. "What if I'm no good to you after a night spent listening to my grandmother and her friends make sex jokes?"

"Then we'll finally have data to prove there really is such a thing as cookie dick," he said.

I wiggled my hips in hopes of rearranging myself without being rude. "So far, so good," I muttered as Darius stepped away to answer one of Nico's questions about his tattoos. "No cookie dick in sight."

After listening to the two of them talk about ink and show off various tattoos, I was even further away from having any dick problems whatsoever. Then Griffin Marian joined the conversation and took off his shirt to show off the giant dragon on his back, and I joined the crew of shameless drooling men standing around gawping.

By the time Darius pulled the truck to a stop outside his house, I was beyond ready to take a tattoo tour of a more private, exclusive nature. A Darius Grant tattoo tour.

"You seem antsy," he said, turning off the ignition. "You sure you're okay staying ov—"

I didn't let him finish his thought. I lunged across the center console and attacked his face with my face.

Cookie dick be damned.

8

DARIUS

There's something to be said for the power of a dark, snowy night only lit by the dim dashboard lights. When Miller surprised me with his kiss, I sucked in a breath for a beat before reaching for his face and holding him close. The kiss was fevered and awkward, made worse by the odd angle across the center console of the truck. But I didn't care about any of that.

Miller Hobbs was warm and sexy, willing… and a damned good kisser.

We made out like teenagers, fogging up the windows and filling the cabin of the truck with groans and stuttered breaths. My hands took advantage of the stolen moment. I grabbed his ass, his back, his shoulders, his hair. I reached for his dick and pressed the heel of my hand down its hard length through his blue jeans.

It wasn't until my hand snuck under his shirt in search of warm skin that he yelped and pulled back. "Cold hands," he gasped with a self-conscious chuckle. "Sorry."

"Let's go inside," I said, quickly opening the door and gesturing to the house. "Much warmer in there."

As soon as I closed the front door behind us, Miller was on me again. His confidence surprised me, but I was as far away from complaining as could be. We grappled across the open floor space toward my bedroom. I peeled off his coat, pulled his shirt out of his pants, and fumbled at the tiny buttons.

"You sure?" I asked against his hot mouth.

"*Gnfh.*"

I tried again through a smile. "Babe, you sure about this? You don't want me to slow down?" I didn't want him to have any regrets.

His answer was to reach up and yank the elastic out of my hair. Messy brown waves tumbled down, forming a curtain around our faces. Miller's fingers went right to my hair, tangling themselves in the locks as if he needed to hold me in place to keep me with him. He didn't.

I was with him. I was with him all the way.

Miller's body was coiled with tension as he wrestled my clothes off. "No slowing down. Very sure."

We finally tripped into my bedroom and fell onto the bed, still half-dressed and trying to kick off our shoes. I didn't want to miss a single moment of discovery. Miller's body had been tempting me all night. His broad shoulders and narrow hips, the way his rounded ass filled out his jeans, and the long stretch of his neck practically begging for my grip... it had all distracted the hell out of me at the lodge. While his family had been busy making merry, I'd been mentally undressing him and doing naughty, naughty things to his naked body.

Miller huffed and pulled at his shirt, which was still caught together by a couple of buttons. I stopped kissing him just long enough to lift it over his head before I pressed him back down on the bed and moved my kisses down the column of his neck to his chest.

After a moment, I heard him let out a sigh, and his entire body seemed to finally relax. "Feels so good," he murmured. His hands were still in my hair, and I loved discovering how much he seemed to enjoy playing with it. His legs wrapped around my back and held me close, and the hard length of his cock pushed into my belly.

"I want to kiss every inch of you," I admitted. "Taste your skin, see your reactions, hear you gasp in pleasure."

He gently yanked my hair until I lifted my head to meet his eyes. "I haven't bottomed for a while, so can we…"

"We don't have to—"

Miller clapped a hand over my mouth so fast I almost snorted with laughter.

"I want to," he said quickly. "I just need some prep."

I kissed his palm. "My pleasure." And I meant it. Hearing he hadn't bottomed for anyone else in a while made me stupidly smug. I'd never been the jealous type before, but for some reason, the idea of Miller Hobbs bottoming for another man made me irritable.

After continuing my kisses down his lightly furred chest to his belly, I reached inside his pants to stroke his cock. Miller arched back and groaned. His frantic pleasure tempted me to tease him, to slow down and draw it out until he was breathless and begging. But I didn't have that much patience tonight.

I wanted inside him. I wanted to see him let go. I wanted to know what it would feel like to be that close to him.

Once I got Miller's clothes off, I grabbed lube and condoms, but before I could prep him with my fingers, I started sucking him off and moved quickly down to rim him as well. He yelped before making a long, drawn-out debauched sound. His fingers stayed tightly gripped in my long hair as I licked and sucked and nipped at him.

He reached for me and wound up twisting us both around until we were sucking each other off and exploring each other's inner thighs, balls, and asses with our mouths.

There was no holding back, no awkward moments of modesty or hesitation. I felt completely at ease with him and more turned on than I could ever remember being.

While Miller had been shy and unsure in the bakery, he was confident and wide open here in bed. His greedy fingers traced every tattoo on my body as if he wanted to memorize them. He was an active and willing participant to the point he verbally resisted me when I tried to pull away and reach for a condom.

"Don't go."

"Grabbing condom," I said, sucking in a breath. "Need you. Can I—"

He didn't even let me finish asking for his consent. Miller immediately nodded. "Yes, fuck yes. Yes."

As soon as I got the condom on and slicked up, I moved between his thighs and reached for a pillow to shove under his hips. Before entering his body, I leaned over and met his eyes. "You are so fucking sexy. So beautiful. Thank you for being here with me tonight."

His eyes widened slightly before his face softened into a smile. "To think I was getting ready to sneak out and leave you with blue balls. Shame you're so damned polite."

As I guided myself into his tight heat, I kept my eyes on his face until I couldn't help but squeeze my eyes closed and hiss. "Fuck, you feel good," I croaked.

Miller's hands held his thighs, but he let go of one to grab the back of my neck and pull me in for a hard kiss. I kept my lips on his as I continued to push into him. By the time I bottomed out, we were both panting and clutching at each other.

He held my face in his hands and wrapped his legs around my back as I began to fuck him, and as I stared down into his hazy blue eyes, the realization washed over me that sex had never been like this for me before. This uninhibited. This connected. This fun. This *right*. In that moment, I knew that he was the only one I wanted to be with like this. Forever.

It completely defied logic to feel that way about someone I'd known for a handful of days. The very idea should have been terrifying.

It wasn't.

The first moment Miller had walked into my bakery, something inside me had whispered, *"This man will be someone important to me."* And sure enough, he already was.

Heck, how could he not be?

His generous heart and open nature showed in the way he loved his outrageous family, even when they sometimes overwhelmed him, and in the way they already doted on him, even though he didn't seem to recognize it. His capacity for loyalty and love was apparent every time he spoke of his mother with raw grief in his voice. And his intelligence and natural curiosity about everything from Greek culture to elaborate cookie decorations fascinated the hell out of me.

Miller deserved a man who'd cherish all the things that made him unique. Who'd spend a lifetime trying to figure him out, and probably never quite get there, but consider every moment well spent anyway.

I was that man.

It didn't make any sense, but I treasured the feeling, nonetheless.

"So beautiful," I murmured against his lips. "Want to stay inside you like this."

"Darius," Miller said with a little hitch in his breath.

"Stay with me," I said without thinking. "Please."

Our eyes met and locked. I thought of the number of times I'd heard people talk about "just knowing" when you'd met the person you were meant to be with. I'd doubted it and had chalked it up to wishful thinking.

But there wasn't a cell in my body that didn't feel like this was finally it. It was my turn to feel the absolute certainty of knowing Miller Hobbs was the one for me.

"Darius," he whispered again, pleading.

I ran my thumbs along the planes of his face, memorizing every freckle and crease. "Want you," I confessed in a broken voice. *More than I've ever wanted anything.*

"I'm yours," he breathed before throwing his head back and letting out a feral sound. I reached down and stroked his dick, murmuring encouragement for him to let go, to come for me.

When his release came, it shattered both of us. I roared into the heated space between us and joined my voice with his.

I hardly knew anything about the man in my arms, but I knew enough. And as far as I was concerned, I had all the time in the world to learn more.

Miller fell asleep as soon as I cleaned him up. When I

followed him under the covers, I wrapped my arms around his boneless form and took a deep, centering breath.

Home.

Months after moving into my dream house, I finally felt like I was truly home.

~

I woke up with a toe almost up my nostril.

"What the hell?" I batted Miller's foot away. "Where did you go?" After cracking open one eye, I spotted him upside down in the bed with one arm hanging down to the floor, the covers twisted around him like an elaborate sari, and his knee draped across my chest.

He was a hot mess, still dead asleep.

"Ngh."

I gently pushed him around until he was the right way around again. His head rested against my shoulder, and he continued to make soft sleeping noises as if he hadn't been bodily manhandled across the bed.

"I now know something about you I didn't know before," I said with a soft chuckle. "You're all sweet and easy until you fall asleep. Then it's every man for his own."

My eyes roamed over his skin, noting adorable freckles here and there I hadn't noticed last night. He had a small scar on his shoulder that had turned white with age, and I noticed a patch of beard that hadn't grown in overnight on the edge of his jaw. I wondered if he'd been the kind of little boy who'd gotten into scrapes or if he'd been careful but had landed himself a few injuries anyway. Noticing these marks only made me want to learn more about his past.

"Babe," I said, nudging him awake enough to hear me. "I have to go to work. It's super early, though. Do you want to stay here?"

"Stay here," he murmured.

"Okay. I can come back after lunch and drive you to the

lodge." I started to climb out of bed, but he tightened the arm he had around me.

"No, you stay here," he said without opening his eyes.

I leaned in and pressed a kiss against his warm, prickly cheek. "I can't. Believe me, I would give anything to stay here with you. But I have holiday orders coming in like crazy at the bakery."

He opened an eye and peered at me. "Oh. Right. I'll come help?"

I brushed the hair back from his face. "You don't have to, but you are always, *always* welcome."

Miller rallied. He got up and let me maneuver him into a hot shower. After resisting all kinds of sexy temptation, I managed to scrub both of us and make us presentable.

We sucked down some coffee on the frigid drive into town, and when I let him into the bakery, he finally seemed to wake up.

"I love this place," he said reverently. "It's so cozy and welcoming."

His words warmed me up inside. "Thank you. That's exactly the kind of place I wanted to create. It's why I waited until I found a storefront with a fireplace. It wasn't easy."

I moved over to start the fire. Hannah might have complained about the work involved in keeping it going all day, but even she admitted what a difference it made to the welcoming feel of the place on cold days.

As soon as the flames began to lick at the wood, I moved into the kitchen, flipped on the lights, and began firing up the ovens.

"It's peaceful in here this time of day," Miller said softly. "Or should I say night?"

I glanced at the darkness outside the shop windows. "It takes some getting used to, but I like the peace and quiet, too."

He moved over to the industrial sink, rolled up his shirt-sleeves, and washed his hands before picking a clean apron off one of the shelves against the wall. "What can I do?"

We spent the next hour measuring ingredients into the large mixing bowl and sharing some of our favorite holiday traditions from growing up. Miller's face lit up when he talked about his mother.

"My mom had this obsession with shortbread, but she'd only eat it during the holidays. She said if she ever allowed herself to eat it during any other month, she'd have a weight and cholesterol problem." He shook his head and sighed despite his soft smile. "Once we knew she wouldn't get better, I ordered her the shortbread stars from Dancing Deer bakery online because they were her favorite. It didn't matter that it was a warm day in spring. We pretended it was Christmas and ate them until we were sick."

I made a mental note to make him some shortbread for Christmas. "My grannie Ruth made a ginger pound cake that was the same way. We could eat that thing until we puked, so she'd only make it at Christmas. One year when I was nine, I overheard my parents talking about Grannie Ruth being sick and possibly not making it till Christmas. The next time I saw her, I shamelessly asked her to make me ginger pound cake for my birthday in case she died before Christmas."

Miller's eyes widened. "No you didn't."

I nodded. "Did too. Needless to say, my mother was horrified. And when Grannie Ruth made me ginger pound cake for my birthday that September, my father clenched his jaw so tightly, I thought his teeth might break. And Grannie simply shot me a wink. She said it had made her feel special when I'd made my request. 'Course, she also implied she'd been planning on giving me a PlayStation 2, but because I'd preferred the cake…" I shrugged. "Served me right. And don't ever play power games with a woman who had eight kids. You won't win."

Miller's laugh filled my kitchen. "I hope that cake was damned good."

"You can tell me when I send one home with you later today," I said, nodding my head toward the Bundt pans I'd prepped on a side table.

We worked together easily, our conversation making the time fly by. When Hannah showed up at six thirty, she was shocked to see Miller there. "Oh, hi," she said, coming to a stop inside the arched opening to the kitchen from the shop. "Did Darius press you into service since we have so much to do today?"

Miller's face flushed pink. "He said you had a lot of holiday orders."

I bit my tongue against a laugh, but Hannah knew me well enough to see right through Miller's blush. "He's not lying," Hannah said with a straight face. "But he has to get here so early in the morning these days, it would have made more sense for you to sleep over if you wanted to get here at the same time."

She turned back and flitted away as Miller groaned and dropped his chin to his chest.

I finally let the laugh go and leaned over to press a kiss to the top of his head. "If only we'd thought of that," I said before ducking down to kiss his warm cheek. "Woman's got a good head on her shoulders."

We eventually settled back into the rhythm of baking as Hannah woke up the shop and began filling the display cases and preparing orders. I noticed Miller's phone buzz several times but refrained from asking why he didn't answer it or even look at it. Finally, I realized who'd been lighting him up...

When it seemed like the entire Marian and Wilde clan showed up as soon as the bakery opened its doors for the day.

9

MILLER

One good thing about growing up without a large family is avoiding the embarrassment that comes with it.

"OMG, there he is!" Otto squealed, making an overly dramatic deal about my presence in the kitchen with Darius.

Sassy put her hands on her hips. "Did he force you to work here? Because I know from experience working in a bakery is no joke. It's like doing hard time, man. Hard. Time."

Rebecca Marian flapped her hand at them. "Hush. Look at that sweet man. He's covered in love dust."

Granny pushed her way to the front. "Pretty sure it's crank or toot. You know… nose candy. Snow." She opened her mouth to say more, but Irene placed her long bony fingers over Granny's flapping jaws to stop her.

Rebecca ignored them. "We're just here to pick up Mikey's order since his regular delivery man is…" She grinned at me. "Otherwise engaged."

"Who got engaged?" Simone said, shoving her brother Blue out of the way. "I'm always the last to know."

I glanced frantically at Darius, who seemed to be taking it all in stride. He had a pleasant grin on his face like this interfering mass was *simply lovely*.

They weren't.

"Gotta go," I said quickly, ripping at the ties on my apron. "Sorry to beat and run."

"What did he say?" Granny asked. "Because it sounded like —" Irene's fingers clapped over Granny's mouth again and stayed there.

I felt my face ignite. "Eggs. Cake batter. Christ."

"One of those things is not like the other," someone muttered.

"Welcome to Honey's," Darius said, wiping his hands off on his own apron before pulling it off and leaving it on a nearby counter. He walked over to help me with mine since I'd managed to tighten the strings into a big knotty mess. "We'll be with you in a moment."

He met my eyes. "Why are you acting like you just got caught with your hand in the cookie jar?" he murmured while he attempted to untangle my strings. "Your family doesn't seem like they're all that prudish."

"You and I have known each other for like two days," I said. "It's... I'm just..."

Darius's smile went from easy to a little forced. "Okay. Fair enough. I didn't mean to push." He pulled the strings loose and stepped back out of my personal space. I leaned forward before catching myself and pulling back. This wasn't the time to sputter an apology for being weird and cagey.

Or to grab him and abscond through the back door.

"You got any of them cookie dicks?" Granny called out. "Because Saint and Otto challenged Griff and Derek to a dick-eating contest, and let's just say *mpfh*."

This time it was Tilly who shut her up. "Let's not," she said calmly, moving Granny into Irene's arms. "Cage your beast."

Tilly turned back to me and gave me a long, assessing look. Her lips curved up slowly like the Grinch. "One must assume you acquired the ultimate cookie dick, Miller. I take it the eating was satisfactory?"

My entire body flushed hot with mortification. "Let's go. I don't want to hold up Mikey's breakfast."

I started to walk out of the kitchen, but Darius stopped me with a gentle throat-clearing. "Don't forget the order."

My eyes closed, and I forced myself to take a deep breath. "Of course." I grabbed the bags we'd already packed and handed them off to a couple of my cousins. "Thank you," I said back to Darius. "I'll…"

His smile was still a little forced, but at least there was warmth in his eyes. "Go. I'll catch up with you later."

"Come to Christmas Eve dinner tomorrow," Tilly said to Darius with her usual tone of regal command. "We shall expect you at six for a seven o'clock meal."

With that, the family swarm turned and moved en masse out of the bakery. I shot Darius an apologetic smile, but it most likely came out as a grimace.

I let the crowd direct me to the passenger vans parked across the street, and I spent the ride up the mountain thinking back on the evening I'd spent in Darius's arms and the morning in his kitchen. Being with him was easy, almost too easy, and for some reason, it made me feel guilty.

I hadn't expected to be happy this soon after losing my mom. As the first holiday season without her, this Christmas was supposed to be something I was meant to *endure*, not enjoy. I'd imagined nights spent alone and sad under a blanket, comfort eating ice cream and pizza, and losing myself in a good thriller novel. Never in a million years had I expected to find myself among this large extended family being distracted from my grief and kept company in spades.

And I'd certainly not anticipated having a holiday fling.

Except "fling" wasn't at all the right word for what was happening between Darius and me. And that scared me even more. How could I finally meet the man I might want to spend forever with when my mom was no longer around to get to know him and tell me what she thought?

When we got back to the lodge, I quickly excused myself and flopped facedown on the bed in my room to have a good cry and talk to my mom.

I miss you so much. You'd like him. He's sweet and easygoing. But also ambitious and hardworking. He's so damned good-looking, and he appreciates family. Also... he seems to think I'm pretty special.

I could almost hear my mom telling me to go for it, to take a chance on Darius.

Kelly Hobbs had been a little quiet and a little shy, but she'd believed strongly in fate and love and happily ever afters, even though my dad had left us for parts unknown when I was still a child. And she'd always, always believed in *me*.

"Miller, honey, you'll find someone who won't love you in spite of the things you perceive as flaws, but because of them," she used to promise me. And I wondered if maybe she was right.

Her endless optimism had made her incredibly resilient, despite how hard she'd had to work to make ends meet as a single mom. It had also made me fiercely protective of her.

I sighed and flopped onto my back after the crying slowed to a trickle. This wasn't fair. It wasn't supposed to be like this. How could I allow myself to be happy right now when the one person I'd always been able to rely on in my life was gone?

My phone buzzed in my pocket. Since I'd finally exchanged numbers with Darius, I secretly hoped he was the one messaging me.

It wasn't Darius. It was my boss.

Kurt: *Went to a cocktail party last night where Bill Hirsch told me about something called Instagram. He said we need to get our advertisements on there. Make a note to look into it when you get back.*

I gritted my teeth and counted to ten. I'd pitched a social media campaign to management—including Kurt—several times in the past year. Every time I had, the team had waved it off as a temporary fad despite the data I had showing otherwise. I'd finally snuck some Facebook and Instagram ads into the budget last quarter and had been running them successfully for several months now.

The results had been on my most recent summary report, very clearly labeled as Facebook and Instagram advertisements.

It didn't surprise me that he finally listened when the head of the local dentistry association said something about it, but it would have been nice for him to trust his own ad executive about it.

Me: *Will do.*

I tossed my phone down on the bedside table and stood up. There was no use in spending time feeling sorry for myself when there was a ginger pound cake out there in Mikey's kitchen waiting to be taste-tested.

After washing my face and straightening my clothes, I went out to embrace the day.

I embraced it for about two hours before things went off the rails again.

"Tiller wants us to test out the ski lift," Jamie Marian explained over a fresh cup of coffee in the sunroom. "They have snow tubes for us, and they've groomed a long easy run for them. I guess they're just getting the ski slopes up and running and need some sacrificial lambs."

Teddy stole Jamie's coffee mug and took a big gulp before adding, "And in true Marian fashion, my beloved husband committed all of us before asking. So off to the slopes we go."

The first run was actually fun. The sun was shining, and the snow was perfect for tubing. I'd never done anything like it before, so I had a few experiences of bumping myself off into the powder before getting the hang of it. It was the second run that did me in.

"*Incoming!*" Derek's warning wasn't enough to prevent me from getting bulldozed by a giant, muscled bodyguard who seemed to be all elbows and boots. I went tumbling over to the side of the run and into a bumpy patch of woods before skidding to a stop on top of some saplings that had never stood a chance against a human torpedo.

"Oh! Oh sh-shoot," Jude said, trying to stop himself in time to help me. Since he had little Wolfe with him, I shot him a half-smile and waved him on. As soon as they disappeared down the slope, I dropped the smile and winced. No big injuries, only lots of little bumps and bruises along with maligned pride.

Finally Maverick and Beau, who'd somehow been meandering at a pace slow enough to keep their hands clasped tightly together, managed to stop and help.

"He's a veterinarian," Beau said proudly but with a hint of teasing in his eyes. "He loves rescuing injured woodland creatures."

"Quiet, you," Mav mumbled before moving off his tube and approaching me. "Anything broken?"

I shook my head. "Just my spirit," I said lamely. "I was feeling pretty cocky there for a while. Thought I had this thing figured out."

"Ah," Beau said. "Pride really does cometh before the fall. Who knew?"

"Goeth," his husband corrected. Maverick helped me stand up and make sure there was nothing seriously wrong with me. Once I'd taken a deep breath and calmed down, I felt well enough to continue down the slope.

"Maybe I should retire after this run and take a restorative nap," I joked.

"Wouldn't be a bad idea," Maverick said. "Especially since you probably didn't get much sleep last night due to all the... *baking*."

I blinked at him at the same time his husband jabbed him in the gut with an elbow. "Manners," Beau warned.

Mav waved his hand in the air. "Dude, he's family. He can take it."

The two of them took off again, argue-flirting like I'd seen many of my other cousins doing. I stared after them with mixed feelings. Was I really family? Technically, yes. According to the DNA, I was most definitely Tilly Marian's biological grandchild. I was as much a Marian as anyone else staying at the lodge this week, and there was no doubt in my mind, Maverick's teasing had been a sign of his acceptance of me.

But that didn't make the good-natured teasing easy for me to take. I had to actively talk myself around it, reminding myself it was meant well and done with affection.

Growing up, our household in Bakersfield had been quiet and peaceful. And for all her sweet, loving nature, my mom had been raised by a conservative adoptive family. While she'd supported me unconditionally when I'd come out, she'd also have burst into flames if I'd ever tried to talk to her about sex, let alone make dick jokes.

"Keeping sex private," she'd said, "is a sign of respect to your partner."

Once I'd gone to college and gotten well-versed in gay culture, I'd dropped some of those uptight traits, but it was still hard for me to get used to sharing my sex life among family. I was trying, but being among the laughing, teasing Marian and Wilde family was like a trial by fire where no subject was inappropriate for sharing in mixed company. They didn't even hold back much from cursing around the kids, and they sure as hell didn't hold back from making dirty jokes around anyone and everyone.

It was taking some getting used to.

But I wanted to get used to it, and I wanted to become more and more comfortable among them. Escaping to my room to nap wasn't the way to go about it, so I vowed to spend quality time with the family instead. As soon as I got back to the lodge, I joined Tilly, Granny, and Harold at the card table for a couple of hours and let Granny spank us all in whist. Thankfully, they didn't try to talk me into trying to play bridge again, because I was terrible at it.

As we sat at the card table in the large sunroom, people came and went, enjoying the now-decorated tree and taking advantage of the table in the corner that still held gift-wrapping supplies.

Outside the windows, snow began to fall in a light flurry. It was the kind of afternoon my mom had always called "a Norman Rockwell day." It had taken me a while to figure out what that meant. Something out of a perfect life or a storybook.

But this was real life, which meant not quite so perfect.

"Did your mom play cards?" Harold asked.

Tilly answered before I could. "She was a junior master in bridge."

Harold glanced at his wife in surprise. "Was she?"

Tilly kept her eyes on her cards. "She said she was active in tournaments until she was married. Only got back into it a few years before she got diagnosed."

Harold seemed upset. "How did I not know this? I spent so much time trying to get to know her."

I cleared my throat. "She didn't like to talk about it since she couldn't play anymore by the time you met her. One of the meds gave her brain fog."

Tilly smiled softly at her cards. "She only mentioned it to me because I was complaining about trying to use the Blackwood convention at a bridge party with absolutely no help from my partner."

Irene spoke up from where she sat crocheting on a nearby sofa. "Which would have been fine if you hadn't claimed to be using ACOL at the beginning of the round."

Tilly ignored her. "We made a small slam on a slam bid. You can imagine my distress. Your mother laughed and suggested hearing aids next time. The gall of that woman."

I choked on the sip of water I'd just taken, and Harold barked out a laugh. "Like mother, like daughter."

Tilly sniffed. "Yes, well, I responded I'd rather get a new partner than fuss with something so unnecessary as hearing aids. I've never had a hard time hearing anyone before. And besides, since when does Blackwood sound like ACOL? Ridiculous."

Harold patted her hand. "There was that one time recently at the gallery opening when you called Marjorie Tudwell 'Margerine' for the better part of ten minutes…"

The look Tilly shot him could have cut glass. "That was a judgment call rather than failed hearing. The woman is slick as a whistle and full of plastic and trans fats."

Harold bit back a laugh and turned away. "Yes, dear."

"Mpfh," Tilly said before taking the next trick.

"She also played Hearts," I added for no reason in particular "And she delighted in sloughing the queen on any unsuspecting idiot regardless of their inexperience with the game."

Granny pointed a finger across the table at Tilly. "J'accuse."

Harold nodded, and Tilly shrugged "Lie down with dogs and

you'll wake up with fleas," she said. "They'll learn quick once those points start adding up."

Granny shot me an unimpressed glance. "She once made Pete and Ginger's daughter cry. Sloughed the queen on her every single hand, over and over, until the girl ran off in tears."

One of the teen girls in question came over and patted Tilly's shoulder. "Thanks to Aunt Tilly, I had six months of therapy. If it hadn't been for that, I may have actually enjoyed my life. No big."

She turned and sauntered off like she hadn't just dropped a bomb on the table. Tilly caught my shocked expression. "She's kidding, Miller. Jeez. The girl's a Marian. She's tough as nails."

When the girl turned and winked at me, I let out a breath.

"You're a horrible woman," I muttered at my grandmother.

Everyone who heard me snickered in agreement while praising Ginger and Pete's daughter for being cool under pressure. Apparently, she and her twin sister had recently competed in a fierce volleyball tournament with their high school and had impressed their coach with their drive to win.

"Is it any surprise when they come from these people?" Blue asked, tilting his head at four of his brothers, who'd turned an innocent game of Jenga into a death match at the nearby coffee table.

I played my card when it was my turn and won the next trick. After I set out the next card, I turned to Blue. "Is there anyone in the family who has a hard time with all of the... competition and... differing personalities?"

Blue studied me for a moment before giving me a knowing look. "You mean the chaos and noise?"

I shrugged. "And the sheer number of people. Surely there are introverts among us."

He nodded. "I think the introverts handle it in different ways. My mom blocks it out and focuses on one person at a time. Jude sits back and watches and lets Derek act as his watchdog. Dante used to get overwhelmed, but after working at Marian House for so long, he's kind of gotten used to it. On the Wilde side... I think Augie and Saint are kind of like Jude and Derek. Saint seems to keep a close eye on Augie to make sure he's not getting bowled over or too agitated. I noticed he tends to make an excuse to take Augie outside or back to their room when things get too chaotic. Grandpa Wilde is more like Dante. It seems like he's gotten used to it over time and actually likes it now. I'm not sure about MJ." Blue directed this last bit at the woman herself.

MJ was stroking her wife's hair while Neckie dozed on MJ's lap. "It wasn't easy growing up," MJ admitted. "It bothered me more then than it does now because I had less control over my life. Neckie has taught me some meditation and breathing techniques that help. We do yoga at home and talk about centering. For a while, in my twenties, I tended to remove myself from stressful situations. There's something to be said for deciding you need space and taking it no matter what everyone else says or thinks. Basically, you need to learn how to look out for you no matter where you are. It's toxic only when you find yourself acting for others' benefit but to *your* detriment."

Her words hit me like an arrow to the chest, and it took me a minute to catch my breath.

"My mom never liked to trouble anyone," I said softly. "She never wanted anyone to know when she was upset. Instead, she tried to focus on the positive, to find the good in people and situations. And she taught me to do the same."

MJ's expression was tender and understanding.

Meanwhile, Tilly huffed. "Well, that's just plain crap. Besides, if you think for one minute your emotions aren't spelled out in bright lights on your face, you're fooling yourself." She adjusted her scarf and pointedly didn't look at me. "Now, it's your turn again, Miller. Play your damned card."

I obeyed without thinking. Later, I realized I'd chosen the easy path rather than argue in defense of my mother.

I regretted it.

Maybe if I'd stood up to Tilly then, things wouldn't have festered. But I hadn't. I'd allowed the moment to pass, and the festering began to feel like molten lava bubbling up in preparation for the inevitable explosion.

10

DARIUS

Maybe I should have felt nervous about joining Miller's big family Christmas dinner, but I didn't. I was overjoyed with the idea of getting to know him better, and since I knew he was still a little uncomfortable around his large family, I hoped my presence would help take some of the focus off him.

Besides which, after spending last night apart, I genuinely missed the man. After just one night in my bed, Miller had left his mark on my space. The place felt a little bit colder without him curled up on my sofa or smiling at me across the kitchen.

When Tiller opened the front door to welcome me inside, I followed the noise to the sunroom down a hallway to the right. Everyone seemed to be gathered around a Christmas tree weighed down with homemade ornaments mixed with store-bought baubles. Strands of cranberries and popcorn wrapped around it, and lights flickered in an unpredictable cadence. It was very representative of the varied group who'd decorated it, and it seemed the perfect tree for the occasion.

"You must be happy to see the lodge filled with so much holiday cheer," I said to Tiller, who'd come into the room after me.

"Mikey is thrilled, which is all I need to be happy. It'll be easier to leave tomorrow night knowing he's in such good company, too."

"You have to get back to Houston for a game?"

I didn't pay close attention to his response when my brain registered Miller wasn't among all the Marians and Wildes in the room.

"I think he went back to his room to find a sweater," one of the cousins said when she saw me craning my neck to look for him. Tiller offered to show me the way to Miller's room and left me standing outside the closed door at the end of a long hallway.

Suddenly, I was unsure.

I knocked lightly. "Miller? It's me. Darius." This was one of those awkward moments when I couldn't help but remember we didn't know each other all that well. Would he want me in his personal space?

I remembered being inside his body two nights ago and realized maybe he'd be okay with me entering his bedroom.

"Come in," he called. I let out a breath and opened the door.

Miller was leaning over the bed to straighten the sheets and comforter. His ass was right in front of me like a tempting slice of cake.

"That's a nice welcome," I murmured, moving closer.

He turned to greet me with a smile. "I was trying to clean up a little in case… in case I had guests over tonight."

"Guests, plural?" I teased, pulling him around and wrapping my arms around him. "My, my, what a naughty boy you are. Does Santa know to bring you a lump of coal tonight?"

Miller leaned in and kissed me. He tasted like my granny's ginger pound cake, which only made me lose yet another piece of my heart to him.

He laughed against my lips. "I was referring to Santa and his reindeer," he informed me. "We usually have a nice cup of tea and a long chat before his final push to Hawaii. I wouldn't want to have a messy room for our visit."

"What if you're not alone when your Christmas friends arrive?" I teased.

He mock frowned. "Why wouldn't I be alone? Although,

now that you mention it, I did get a funny feeling from Mikey and Tiller's friend Lorenzo..." He blinked at me. "Maybe you're right. You think Lorenzo might want to sleep over? I could ask him. His muscles might be a little too big to fit in this bed, but *hngh*!" I shut him up with a hard kiss to his mouth and clenched his hair in my fist as I held his head and devoured him.

The little breathy whimper sounds only encouraged me to deepen the kiss until we were both half-dressed and all the pristine bedding was in a heap on the floor.

When we finally came to our senses after a quick, humping frot, Miller eyed me sheepishly. "Jealousy looks good on you."

I snorted. I'd never considered myself a jealous person before, but it seemed all bets were off when it came to Miller Hobbs. "Duly noted."

We made our way to the public area of the lodge just as Tiller was leading everyone outside into a clear path cut through the snowy backyard. A large event tent was set up at the end of the lantern-lit path, and inside were enough gas heaters to make the place surprisingly comfortable.

Everyone gasped as we took in the gorgeous setup. Half of the tent was a long dining table set with gorgeous evergreen floral arrangements and sparkling crystal. The other half sported a small stage and wooden dance floor. A cluster of musicians was set up on the stage, warming up their instruments, and several uniformed servers were already passing around trays of champagne glasses.

I lifted an eyebrow at Miller. "Did you know...?" He shook his head aggressively.

"No. I had no idea. Tilly must have arranged it."

Sure enough, Miller's grandmother looked happily satisfied with the results as she leaned her head in to murmur something to Tiller. Tiller nodded and led Tilly over to the stage, where he gestured to a microphone. Harry stepped up next to her in silent support.

"Pfft, I don't need that," she said, growing loud enough to begin gathering everyone's attention. "Listen up, everyone. I wanted to do something special to celebrate this gathering of

friends and family. As you all probably know, family means…"
She cleared her throat and waved away Harold's attempt to
comfort her. "A lot to me. And what better way to celebrate ours
than with a decadent shared meal and some caroling and dancing? I'm not going to prattle on, but I wanted to invite everyone
to kick back, eat up, sing your heart out, dance your feet off, and
enjoy this rare moment in time when as many Wildes and
Marians are gathered together as possible."

Everyone held their glasses up to join her in a toast that was
quickly followed by cheering. Some of the parents of little kids
pulled them onto the dance floor to show them some steps, and
the rest of us stood around talking and drinking while the live
music started.

It was a lovely night full of celebration. I pulled Miller onto
the dance floor as soon as a tune began that lent itself to the
moves I knew.

"Swing?" Miller asked in surprise when I moved him
through the steps.

"I took a few classes with some of my friends at culinary
school. They were cheap since our group was willing to go in the
middle of a workday," I added. "Unfortunately, when you work
in the food industry, you miss out on the good nightlife. You're
either working nights and weekends or working so early in the
morning, you're in bed by eight."

Miller was a good dancer and knew how to follow my lead. It
made me naturally curious about who he'd danced with before. I
bit my tongue to keep from asking since I knew I wouldn't be
able to say it without sounding like a jealous ass for the second
time in one evening.

I'd never felt as possessive of Clay as I already did of Miller.
Why was that? And was it a bad sign of some kind?

"Rebecca Marian keeps a close eye on you," I said, noticing
the woman smiling affectionately at us from where she danced
with her husband.

"She reminds me of my mom. She's very kind and attentive."
The emotion was clear in Miller's voice, but I sensed the dance

floor wasn't the place he wanted to reveal it. I dropped the subject and moved to something else.

"I heard you guys went tubing. Was it fun?"

That did the trick. Miller's face lit up as he told me about the sensation of flying down the mountain and watching his cousins do the same.

"I think I might want to come back here when the slopes open for skiing and take a few lessons," he said, avoiding eye contact with me.

I moved a finger under his chin and lifted it up so he was forced to look at me. "You'll stay with me when you do," I said softly but firmly. "Okay?"

His rosy lips widened into a big smile. "If you insist."

We talked about Mikey and Tiller's plans for the ski resort as we continued our dance. When the song ended, I moved us off the dance floor and over to a cluster of Miller's cousins, where I recognized the tattoo artist I'd talked to the other night.

"Nico, good to see you again."

The ink-covered man reached out a hand to shake. "You too. Merry Christmas Eve. Glad you could make it."

As we picked up our conversation about ink from the other night, I felt the smooth slide of Miller's hand in mine. I glanced over to find him listening to his cousin Sassy. She spoke animatedly about Miller's work with me in the bakery, asking him questions about how I worked and what kind of equipment we had in the kitchen. Miller replied in short nods and one-word answers like he was distracted, and I wondered if he was thinking of his mom. Rather than butting into the conversation, I squeezed Miller's hand lightly in support, then turned back to Nico and asked him more questions about a design we'd begun discussing.

"Do you ever travel for commission work?" I asked.

His eyes widened. "Well, yeah, but it's usually for celebrities and shit. I charge an arm and a leg."

His husband leaned in. "He doesn't trust me alone with the girls."

Nico rolled his eyes. "Okay, well... he's not lying. Still. It's a little rich for the average Joe."

Tilly must have overheard because she murmured something in his ear before walking away again. Nico's eyes met mine. "You own Dough?"

I shot a quick glance at Miller to see his reaction, but he hadn't heard. He was still busy talking to Sassy.

"Not anymore," I explained. "I sold it almost a year ago."

West's forehead crinkled. "Wasn't that the place you took me to in New Orleans? The one we had to stand in line for?"

Nico nodded. "The fastest-growing bakery chain in America. It started in Chicago and spread like wildfire. How many locations did you have when you sold it?"

"Twenty-six."

West whistled, but Nico's face creased in concern. "How the hell did you manage all that?"

"Poorly," I said with a laugh. "Hence the sale. I hated it. Growing it like that was the biggest mistake I could have made. It took all the joy out of it. I went from spending happy time in the kitchen to spending miserable time around a boardroom table. It was a high-pressure way to learn a lot of lessons very fast."

I felt the squeeze of Miller's hand in mine. "I didn't know any of that," he said in surprise. Obviously, he'd tuned in enough to catch the gist of things.

I glanced over at him, wondering if I should apologize for some reason. "No, I didn't mention it earlier. I didn't want you to..."

Think of me differently.

Have high expectations of me.

Choose me only because of what I've done rather than who I am.

"Think it was weird," I finished lamely. "That I'd rather have one small bakery in Aster Valley than this large chain all over the country."

Thankfully, Nico, West, and Sassy had made themselves scarce so Miller and I could speak openly.

"I would never think it was weird to want to follow your passion," he said with a scowl. "I'm upset you'd think that of me. How could you think I'd want you to be unhappy?"

100

His annoyance surprised me. "I didn't," I said quickly. "Of course I didn't. It's just awkward. How do you tell someone you sold a multimillion-dollar business without sounding like a braggart?"

Miller sighed. "Yeah. I get that. I just... feel like I missed something huge, especially if you've been through all of this in the past year. It must have been a stressful transition."

Before I could answer, he continued. "And how the hell did my grandmother know before I did?"

He seemed oddly disgruntled by this. I opened my mouth to explain it had been national news at the time and maybe she recognized my name, but I realized I would have been talking to nothing but Miller-shaped air.

Because the man himself had turned around and stormed off, leaving me behind.

11

MILLER

Ever since the card game the day before—or maybe longer than that—I'd been having unkind thoughts about my grandmother.

Tilly was everyone's favorite, the matriarch of this large collection of truly special people.

She was a wonderful woman in many ways. She was educated and refined, polite but also fascinatingly irreverent. Matilda Marian was known for her generosity around the Bay Area, and Rebecca had once told me proudly that Tilly gave even more money away anonymously. Marian House, the home for LGBTQ+ youth that Dante ran, was financed in large part by donations from Tilly's trust.

But Tilly was also the woman who'd left my mother behind. She'd never looked for her, even when she'd had the resources to do so, and then had refused to see her at first, even when she found out my mom was terminally ill. And no matter how much good Tilly did for the world, none of that could undo the devastated expression on my mom's face when she'd gotten the news her biological mother hadn't wanted to meet her.

Yes, Tilly had eventually changed her mind, and they'd gotten to spend plenty of time together before my mom's death. And yes, my mom had forgiven her because that was the kind of amazing person my mother was. But I hadn't been quite able to manage forgiveness yet.

So when Tilly had dared to suggest during the card game that my mother had been wrong to be selfless and look for the good in people—the very qualities that had led her to forgive Tilly in the first place, for goodness' sake!—it had sparked resentment that had been smoldering inside my chest ever since.

Tonight, while everyone had cheered and held up their glasses to Tilly, all I'd been able to think was that my mother, whose dying wish had been to reconnect with the family who'd abandoned her, had never been able to witness this large gathering of her extended family because of Tilly's selfishness. And that smoldering resentment had flared hotter.

Tilly got to stand up there in front of this huge family and hold court, claiming that family meant a lot to her?

Bullshit.

If family meant so much to her, where the hell had she been when my mother was trying her hardest to hold on long enough to meet her? It was only by the luck of an experimental treatment Mom had ended up with the four extra months at the end to finally get to know her biological parents. Tilly had almost missed it because of her stubborn selfishness and fear.

I understood her reasons for giving my mom up as a baby. But how could Tilly give up her child a second time, at the end of her life when she was sick and needed her?

And then to find out that my grandmother knew more about my… my… *Darius* than I did?

That was the final straw that got the flames in my chest burning like a Christmas bonfire.

Typical Tilly, always needing to know everything. It reminded me of the time when Tilly showed up for a visit to my mom's house and tried talking her into a new experimental treatment. She'd somehow gotten her hands on my mother's hospital records—despite every privacy law known to man—and thought she knew better than the doctors what was best for my mother's cancer. She was a meddling, interfering control freak.

Without thinking, I made a beeline for Tilly. She stood in the center of the tent between the dining and dancing areas, talking to Blue and Simone.

"How did you know about Darius's company?" I blurted.

Tilly studied me for a beat. "Google."

I bit my teeth to keep from snapping at her while air sawed in and out of my nose. "And what business is it of yours? Why were you looking for information about him?"

She stood up even straighter than normal, and her face lifted in her usual imperial glare. "I wanted to look out for the safety and well-being of my grandchild."

I made a disbelieving sound. "Right. As if you care. As if you ever cared."

Blue stepped forward with a look of true concern on his face. "Miller—"

I held up a hand to stop him. "Don't. This is between me and Tilly. She's strong enough to defend herself."

"I'm more concerned about protecting you from her," Blue said, looking back and forth between us.

Tilly made a shooing gesture with her long fingers. "Leave us be. He's right, and Miller obviously has some things he'd like to get off his chest."

Blue stayed right where he was and folded his arms across his chest. I ignored him.

"I don't understand you," I informed her. "Why do you want me here? Is it all for show? Give your long-lost grandson a decent Christmas and absolve yourself of any guilt for what happened to his mom? Because you've made a big deal about inviting me here, and you made that pretty speech up there about family, but you and I both know that you couldn't be bothered to come see—" I sucked in a breath just as my voice broke.

Strong, warm arms wrapped around me from behind.

"Walk with me," Darius murmured. "This isn't the place or the time for a confrontation. Let everyone enjoy their Christmas Eve celebration. Dinner is ready."

Tears smarted in my eyes as I realized he was right. No, it wasn't his place to call me down for my behavior, but I was grateful anyway. "Yeah," I whispered. "Okay."

I didn't look at Tilly. Instead, I let Darius lead me across the tent and out into the frigid night air. The sharp sting of it on my heated face made my eyes water even more.

Darius began to apologize for interfering, but I cut him off with a kiss. I grabbed the sides of his face and lost myself in kissing him for just a minute.

All I needed was a minute.

His arms came around me and held me tight as I assaulted his mouth and clasped his face. Even as I was kissing him, I was saying a silent prayer of thanks for him. I was grateful for his steady presence, for feeling like I had someone on my side when it felt like everyone else was here for Tilly.

I pulled myself away. "I'm so angry," I croaked. "I'm so fucking angry, and I can't... I can't hold it in any longer."

"You don't have to," he said gently. "Let it out. Lean on me. Say what you want to say. I can take it. I promise."

I could see the sincerity in his eyes. He truly meant it. Even though we barely knew each other, he was willing to carry my burden for a little while.

"She left my mom all alone in that place, the home for unwed mothers. And I get it, I do. I know she was young and afraid. I know she didn't have options, and if she'd kept my mom, it wouldn't have been a good life for either of them. But later... she had years to find my mom, Darius. Years after my mom's adoptive parents died, when my mom was all alone in the world. Years when my mom was stuck in a crappy marriage. Years when it was just her and me, and she was working two jobs so I could have a good life. And then when we found her, when Tilly was already rich and settled, confident and happy, and all my mom wanted was to know her... Tilly left her all over again. Refused to see her until Grandpa and Harold talked her into it. How, Darius? How could she do that to my mom of all people, when my mom was the sweetest, most loving person?"

I cried into the crook of his neck, clinging onto his soft sweater and taking comfort in the familiar scent of his skin. Darius's large hands rubbed circles on my back as he murmured soothing sounds in my ear.

"I'm so sorry you're hurting. I can't imagine how much you miss her. She must have been incredible to have raised such a caring, considerate, beautiful son."

His words made my stomach feel light and fluttery, but I could tell Darius was frustrated he couldn't give me more specific words of wisdom about the situation. He didn't know enough of our family history to truly understand my resentment, but having the comfort of his embrace was enough to calm me down. When the tears stopped, I took a deep breath and reached down for some snow to wash my face off with. I was freezing by then, out of the warm radius of the gas heaters inside the tent.

"Sorry I brought you out here to die of hypothermia," I teased lamely as I threw the melty snow remnants down and shook off my hands.

"You're worth the loss of a few digits." Darius winked at me and offered me an actual linen handkerchief.

"Where the hell did you get that?" I asked. "1954?"

He looked sheepish. "I actually get nosebleeds because of the altitude. When I tried carrying tissues around, I inevitably ended up running them through the washing machine and making a mess. My mom sent me these for my birthday."

I looked a little closer and saw a tiny embroidered cupcake in the corner of the handkerchief. My heart squeezed. "That's the sweetest thing ever. She must have loved stitching this for you."

Darius laughed softly. "She totally would have if she hadn't been too busy launching a new version of the HR software she manages. It's more likely she found someone on the internet to do the stitching. But it's the thought that counts, right?"

I couldn't help but snort out a laugh, even though I wasn't sure if it was funny or not. "Do you get a chance to see her very often?"

Darius took my hand to lead me back inside the tent, where we took our seats partway down one side of the long table. "I went back to Chicago for Thanksgiving with the family a few weeks ago. And she was here in the summer helping me decorate my house. When I lived in the city, she helped me grow the business, so I saw her plenty. I have two sisters back in Illinois that keep her pretty busy with grandchildren."

As Darius continued to tell me about his mom and the rest of his family, I was torn between being happy for him and sad for me, which only served to make me feel like a selfish asshole. What kind of monster couldn't simply be happy to hear about someone's warm and loving family? Me, apparently.

I wished it had been *my* mom who'd helped *me* run a business. I wanted it to be *my* mom who'd been so busy living her big life that she had to outsource a handmade gift. And I needed it to be *my* mom who hosted Thanksgiving dinner and made sure I came home for it.

A burst of laughter from farther down the table caught my attention. Smiling faces shone behind sparkling crystal wineglasses, and it was clear everyone was having a nice time. The fact I was feeling sorry for myself instead of celebrating with everyone else made me feel like the worst kind of ungrateful human.

I turned to Darius. "I'm sorry I'm such poor company. I didn't expect... well, scratch that. I knew this holiday was going to be hard for me without my mom, but I didn't mean for you to witness it. I don't want to ruin your holiday, too."

His eyes held warmth and understanding, which helped me finally let go of some of my stress. "Miller, you're allowed to grieve, even if it happens on Christmas Eve. And you're not ruining anything for me. If it wasn't for you, I'd be at home by myself watching Christmas movies with a frozen pizza."

Sam Marian sucked in a breath on Darius's other side. "I didn't mean to eavesdrop, but dear god. Frozen pizza on Christmas? Don't do me like that, man."

"He's a chef," I said to Darius in a stage whisper. "You know how they are."

Darius and Sam both laughed and began swapping culinary stories. I let out a breath and sat back. The food Mikey had lovingly prepared for us was delicious, but my appetite was virtually nonexistent. My stomach was tied up in knots. I didn't want to be angry and resentful toward Tilly, but even after venting to Darius, I couldn't seem to shake these feelings. After everything that had happened with my mom, I hadn't had the emotional energy to tackle the "Tilly situation" for a while. But now it seemed my subconscious was serving it up to me on a silver platter.

I took another deep breath and tried to talk myself out of this funk. The Marians and Wildes surrounding me were truly some of the best people I'd ever known. They'd gone out of their way to include me and make me feel welcome in the family. With this many new family members, I should have been grateful. It was an embarrassment of riches.

And I *was* grateful. I reached for my wineglass and took a sip of the soft, oaky cabernet. Blue and Tristan had shipped wine from their vineyard to supply the events of the week here at the lodge. Sam and Griff had treated all of us to a lovely brunch earlier in the day at a diner in town they'd rented out for the occasion. Dante and AJ knew the family who owned it as they'd adopted their son through Marian House. While we were strolling through the small town square, Jude had stopped to sign autographs for everyone who'd asked.

These were generous, loving people. For the most part, they modeled exceptional, giving behavior. They inspired me to want to be the same way, positive and generous.

See? I'm looking for the good, Mom, I thought, and I felt some of my tension melt away.

Even Darius was sporting an extra halo tonight now that I'd heard the story of him selling his business to pursue a quieter life. It explained so much. His incredible showpiece of a home, his easy mood at the bakery despite the holiday orders piling up, and his willingness to leave it behind and enjoy time with new friends, despite this being a busy time for his business.

I was encouraged and inspired by his active pursuit of a better work-life balance, and since I felt like I was at a cross-roads in my own life, the example was timely.

Around the table, there were so many examples of successful entrepreneurs and family-owned businesses. Nico's tattoo shop, Charlie's pub, Augie's antique shop, Tristan and Blue's vineyard, and Sam's restaurant on-site. Teddy's photography business, Maverick's veterinary practice, and Beau's contractor firm. It occurred to me I'd have a bastion of support if I decided to start something of my own.

Since AJ's dad was sitting on my right and he lived in Aster Valley, I decided to ask him more about the town. "What made you and Mrs. Flores decide to settle in Aster Valley? You started off in Chicago, originally, right?"

The older man had a kind smile and laugh lines by his eyes. "Right. But our teenager was getting into trouble at school, so we decided to change our lifestyle and move him to a much safer environment."

I glanced in surprise at AJ several places down the table. He was laughing at something Hallie Wilde was saying. "AJ, you mean? You're kidding. He's such a straight-arrow now. The change must have worked."

"It wasn't that easy. He ran away as soon as we got here." AJ's dad chuckled. "But you're right. Eventually he adapted and started to love it here, just as we'd hoped he would. As for why Aster Valley... I was friends with the people who used to own this lodge, and they'd been in the area a long time. They recommended Aster Valley as a nice place to raise a family. They were right."

"Must've been a huge change," I mused.

"It was, but it became home really quickly. Now we're thrilled to see Mikey and Tiller bringing back the ski resort. It's going to bring in quite a bit of job opportunities and tax revenue, which will help the city planners with some of the projects they've cooked up. Now that I'm retired, I've signed on to help. Several of us who've been here a while are trying to make sure the growth is controlled and we continue to be a nice place to live and visit."

We talked for a little longer about the town of Aster Valley and the small businesses moving into the area in anticipation of the new resort. It sounded like there would be a lot of opportunity for small-town marketing consulting if there wasn't already someone here doing it.

I glanced back at Darius and wondered if I was being presumptuous. Was it shortsighted to consider moving to a place I'd only been to once? Would he think me too forward? Would he even be interested in having me around that long?

"AJ tells me you work for an orthodontist?" Mr. Flores asked.

"I manage marketing and advertising for a chain of orthodontist offices in Monterey," I explained. "But I took that job to be close to my mom while she was sick. Now that she's gone, I've been considering a change." Ideally, one where I wouldn't have to work multiple jobs.

He nodded pensively. "Well, I know there's a high demand for people who are knowledgeable about that sort of thing. Mikey and Tiller have had a heck of a time finding someone to help with branding at the resort."

I stared at him. "Really?"

He nodded. "If you know of anyone, maybe you could give them a heads-up? I know when Mikey asked Tilly whether you'd ever consider taking on clients here, she was adamant that you'd never want to move out of California, so you don't have to worry that he'll pressure you, no matter how much he'd like to, but you might…"

I didn't hear the rest of his sentence through the sudden roaring in my head. "I'm… I'm sorry, she what? Tilly told Mikey I'd never want to leave California?"

"He asked her if she thought he should approach you about the job, and she said not to. That you were happy where you were and didn't need the money anyway. I don't know if she was implying your mother had left you an inheritance or not." He shrugged uncomfortably.

I felt light-headed. Not only had my mother not left me an inheritance, she'd left me with significant debt that had wiped out my own savings account and forced me to take on extra work. While I enjoyed the freelance stuff I was doing, the long hours had worn me down. How dare she imply I didn't need money? How dare she turn down an interesting opportunity without allowing me to make my own decision? How dare she think she knew what was best for me when she hardly knew me at all?

The light from the candles on the table and the fairy lights strung overhead sparkled off Tilly's jewelry. She was obviously extremely wealthy. Her home in Nob Hill alone had to be worth ten million dollars, and she had a personal butler and driver. My mom and I had never asked her for a dime, and in fact, we'd declined all of Harold and Tilly's offers of financial support. But Tilly had no idea what my bank balance looked like or how much money I owed. She didn't even know what I wanted to do with the rest of my life because she'd never asked.

"I think I'll ask Mikey about it," I said with a forced smile. "Thank you for mentioning it. Working on the resort sounds like a dream job."

His face widened in a genuine smile. "Well, we'd certainly love to help welcome you to town, and I'm sure we could find you some guys who play Ultimate Frisbee around here. Dante told me you'd promised to teach him how to play. I know he'd love that."

This extended family really was filled with the nicest people on the planet... along with one octogenarian know-it-all.

"Thank you. I'd love that. It's certainly a lot to consider, but maybe Dante would be better off learning Ultimate with me in California rather than snowy Colorado."

We continued talking into the main course, and I learned more about the interesting work AJ and his dad had done for years. Now it seemed AJ focused his personnel extraction skills on pulling LGBTQ+ youth out of dangerous situations and working with Dante to keep them safe once they were out.

"They wouldn't be able to do half of what they do without your grandmother's help," he said. "Such kindness. Such concern for saving those kids and making sure they have a good, safe life. She's been an incredibly generous benefactor to the program, as I'm sure you've heard, and—"

I didn't listen to any more praise for Tilly's generosity. MJ's words from the other day reverberated in my memory.

There's something to be said for deciding you need space and taking it no matter what everyone else says or thinks. Basically, you need to learn how to look out for you no matter where you are.

The lovely Christmas Eve celebration that Mikey and Tiller had worked so hard to put on for our family was in full swing. It was everything I would have ever wanted had I been able to order up my dream family celebration as a lonely only child. The decorations were gorgeous, the food was delicious. Everyone around me was happy and welcoming.

And I was absolutely miserable. Even the warm, steady presence of Darius next to me couldn't stop me from this plummeting cycle of bitterness and negativity.

I missed my mother so badly my chest felt like it would collapse from the weight of it. As wonderful as most of the Wildes and Marians were, and as promising as my relationship with Darius seemed, there was no comforting familiarity here. These people had been in my life for a year—the worst year of my life—but they didn't really know me yet. They didn't know about the preschool paper snowman decorations that my mother had proudly trotted out every December for twenty-five years or how she'd cha-cha around the kitchen, butchering the words to "Feliz Navidad" while she cooked. They didn't know she'd cried happy tears every single Christmas Eve when George Bailey realized he'd lived a wonderful life.

It felt ungrateful to yearn for those simple Christmas memories when I was surrounded by such beauty and love. But it also felt wrong to enjoy all the beauty without grieving for the holidays I'd never have again.

One thing I knew for sure, though, was that I didn't want to bring anyone else down the bitterness and negativity spiral with me.

I murmured an excuse to Mr. Flores and turned to Darius, wishing like hell I could keep the tears from coming until I was out of the tent.

"I'm so sorry," I breathed. "I can't stay here."

Darius shoved back his chair. Clearly, he intended to come with me. I shook my head and tried to tell him with my eyes how sorry I was, but I needed to be alone. He seemed to understand right away, which only made me like him more.

"Go," he said softly. "Do what you need to do. I am here for as much or as little of it as you want. If you need me, I'll be here. Do you understand?"

I nodded and reached out to squeeze his hand before making my way out of the tent and into the starless night.

12

DARIUS

When Miller exited the tent, I looked toward his grandmother to see if she noticed. While I knew she was a big part of the reason he was so upset, I hadn't been around long enough to understand the nuances of this family dynamic.

She watched him go with a narrowing of her eyes. Once he was out of sight, she turned to look at me. I lifted my eyebrows as if to say, *What are you going to do about it?*

She frowned and pushed her chair back before coming over to speak to me. "Where's he going?"

"Away," I said calmly even though I wanted to blame someone for his mood and she seemed the easiest target after everything he'd told me. "I think he needs some air. I'm sure being here is bittersweet for him after losing his mom."

Tilly's eyes shifted from me to the door of the large tent and back. I could tell she was worried, and I assumed she was trying to decide whether to go after him or not. I pulled out his empty chair and gestured for her to take a seat.

"Why don't you give him a minute to catch his breath and calm down?"

She clasped her hands primly in her lap. The black velvet jacket she wore sported a lovely diamond-and-ruby pin in the

114

shape of a candy cane, and her makeup was pristine. She looked like money and elegance rolled into one haughty package.

All except the slight tremble in her hands.

I'd been watching her. After seeing how worried Miller had been about her at the police station, I'd quickly realized how important she was to him, even if his affection for her was twisted up with resentment. He'd been truly worried about her even though it had seemed from everyone else's reaction this type of prank behavior was commonplace for Tilly and her friends.

From what I'd observed, she was generally as steady as a steel warship plowing through deep waters. But after the run-in with Miller tonight, she was clearly upset.

She reached toward Miller's plate and pushed it away from the edge of the table before straightening the silverware he hadn't used yet. "He misses her," she said absently.

"Very much," I agreed.

Her eyes flicked to me before quickly returning to the place setting she was fussing with. "He blames me."

I didn't respond. Not only was it not my place to agree or disagree, it didn't seem like she was expecting me to say anything.

She moved his wineglass half an inch to the right and then slid it back. "I don't know how much he's told you, but..." Her eyes met mine again for a split second. It was off-putting to see such a normally composed woman seem so unsure of herself. I noticed her husband glancing worriedly at her from down the table. "I got pregnant with his mother when I was a teenager."

I nodded, and she waved her hand before continuing. "Of course, you knew that part from what he said earlier. But what you may not know is that I don't regret giving her up." She stiffened her jaw and met my eyes in a challenging glare. "Giving her up was the best thing for both of us."

"I don't think he blames you for giving her up when you were practically a child yourself," I said.

"No," she admitted, looking away again. Harold must have met her eye because she made the same hand flap gesture but directed it at him this time. He frowned, and she sighed. "Miller blames me for refusing to see her when he first told me she was sick."

It was hard to hear her over the noise around the table. She spoke softly, almost to herself. I didn't say anything. Her hands continued to tremble.

"He's right to blame me," she said. "I… I was…"

I reached out and put my hand on her arm. The velvet sleeve felt as soft as it looked, but her arm felt frail beneath the luxurious fabric. "I think maybe you should be saying this to him," I offered gently.

She closed her eyes for a moment before flashing me a surprising smile. "But it's much easier to say it to you."

I acknowledged her point with a low chuckle before pushing back my chair. "True, but I'm heading home. Christmas is a time to be together with family. I promised mine I'd do a video call tonight, and if I call early enough, I might be able to watch my nephews open their presents."

Tilly reached out and clasped my hand. "Can I talk you into staying a little longer? In case… in case he wants someone to talk to that's not…" She gestured grandly at the long table full of laughing, chatting Marians and Wildes. "Family."

I leaned in and kissed her cheek. "There's a lot I don't know about Miller and this situation, Tilly, but the one thing I do know is that family is exactly what he needs, whether he realizes it or not. *You* are what he needs. Talk to him. Tell him you love him. Tell him you're scared. He can take it."

Her eyes widened in surprised when I said the "*J*" word, but she didn't argue with me. She let me press a kiss to her cheek and patted my arm distractedly.

I waved my hand at a few of the family members who noticed my departure, and I clapped Sam Marian on the back with a murmured "Merry Christmas."

When I left the tent, Miller was nowhere to be found, which I'd expected. Shoe prints in the snow led away from the house toward the trees bordering the ski slope, and I could see the faint pinprick of light from his cellphone in the distance.

He would be okay. He had an entire party tent full of people who would make sure of it, and my number in his phone if he ended up needing a rescue.

I walked around the side of the house and slid into the freezing-cold cab of my truck. The cold air was bracing, but it invigorated me for the dark drive home. As I drove through Aster Valley, I saw very few cars on the road. Most people were already settled somewhere safe and warm for the night, celebrating with friends and family.

Even though I was all by myself, I was happy and relaxed. It had been easier than I expected walking away from the Marian and Wilde family dinner.

Because I felt deep down inside it would be the last Christmas Eve I'd spend by myself.

After seeing the easy way Miller had turned to me for comfort when he was upset, I'd known, *just known*, we were meant to be together. I was falling for him so quickly and so hard, it should have set off alarm bells.

But it didn't.

When I got home, I lit a fire and turned on a few lamps before pouring myself a glass of wine and bringing my laptop over to the sofa.

My mom answered the video call on the first ring. "Merry Christmas Eve!" she said. "Even though *real* Christmas isn't for a while yet…"

"Don't act like you follow the Greek Orthodox calendar anymore," I said, grinning from ear to ear at her familiar joke. "Unless Yaya is there eavesdropping."

She winced. "Wash your mouth out, Darius Grant."

"Where is everyone?" I asked. From the background, it looked like she was in her bedroom.

"They're in the living room hanging stockings. I just came back here to change out of my shoes. I thought you said you were going to wait and call tomorrow? Your sister said you were going to a dinner somewhere."

I leaned back on the sofa and settled in. "I did. It was lovely, but I left early."

She frowned. "I'm sorry to hear that. It's not too late to catch a flight home, you know."

I felt my grin coming back. "I am home, Mom."

I could tell from her expression she was unsure what to make of my words. "You seem happy," she said.

"I am."

"And?" she prodded.

"Remember the other day when I said when there was something to tell, I'd let you know?"

Her eyes widened, and she sat down on the end of her bed before asking, "Yes?"

"There's something to tell. His name is Miller Hobbs."

13

MILLER

I left the tent with only a little jangle of nerves about Darius's reaction. I felt guilty for leaving him in the middle of such a nice event, and I felt even worse for leaving him alone with a bunch of strangers on Christmas Eve. But it was like every moment of grief that I'd pushed down for the past year of my mother's illness and death had come boiling up to the surface, and I felt like it was going to erupt all over him—and anyone else near me —if I stayed there any longer.

I loved that he'd seen that. That he'd understood without words something that even I didn't fully understand.

The cold air was welcome at first. It tempered my hot skin and allowed me to take deep, cleansing breaths as I walked toward the woods. The moon was a hazy smudge of light behind a thick band of clouds, but there was enough of it reflecting off the snow to allow me to make my way to the tree line, where I could catch a glimpse the smooth, groomed ski run beyond.

The mountainside was peaceful. I wondered what the bare slope would look like once the resort opened to skiing. Right now, it was eerily silent, but I could imagine it full of colorful parkas, skis, and snowboards as happy people threw themselves down the mountain at top speed.

I used the flashlight on my phone to pick my way through the trees until I stood at the edge of the slope.

There was something meditative about looking out at the expansive winter night. I continued taking deep breaths of the frozen air and even enjoyed the chill on my nose and cheeks.

Visions of my mom flooded my mind.

You would have loved it here. So peaceful and beautiful.

I closed my eyes and remembered the first time I'd seen snow. Before my dad had left, we'd gone on a long road trip to visit his family in Salt Lake City. My mom had bundled me up in a hand-me-down snowsuit someone had loaned her, and we'd gone out to make a snowman in my grandparents' backyard. The memory of her pink cheeks and bright eyes was as clear as the winter sky, so clear it made me wish I knew how to sketch so I could capture it on paper.

"It's a snowman superhero," she'd said, indulging my recent obsession with all things Marvel. She'd even found an old red towel and pinned it on the snowman's shoulders as a cape.

Another memory pushed that one away. Her leaving me with those grandparents so she and my dad could go out for the night. I'd cried at being left with practical strangers, and I'd begged her not to leave me alone with them.

She'd snapped at me and told me not to be selfish, that she deserved a time-out from being a mom every once in a while.

I remembered feeling devastated. As a child, I'd interpreted it to mean she saw being my mom as a job. Obviously now, I saw it in a different light. Of course she'd deserved a break from taking care of a small child, and she was probably stressed and desperate for a break from her in-laws, too.

The memory was my subconscious's gentle reminder she wasn't perfect. No one was. But I didn't want to fall into the trap of sugarcoating her memory. She was fallible, she was human. I simply missed her.

When the cold seeped through my clothes, I turned and made my way back to the house. The Christmas tree lights shone through the glass wall of the sunroom, beckoning me to the cozy space when I finally made my way into the warm house.

The fire was dying in the fireplace, so I added a couple more logs and poked at it with the heavy metal tool.

"Where did you learn to feed a fire?"

I turned to see Tilly. Whenever she entered a room, I was always struck by her regal bearing. Tonight, she was resplendent in a velvet-and-satin pantsuit. Her hair was coiffed perfectly, and the only thing out of place seemed to be the pink tip of her nose from the cold.

"Camping trip with a local bear club," I said without thinking.

She looked confused. "Bear cl... oh."

"Yeah, that kind of bear. I went through a lumberjack phase a few years back. I couldn't even tell you why. I hate camping. Learned that the hard way." I put the poker back in its stand and took a seat on the nearest sofa.

Tilly picked her way through the various toys left in the room until she took her place on the other end of the sofa. Even though I'd assumed our next conversation would be awkward and strained, now that we were here together, the air between us was simply sad. Or maybe that was just me. My earlier resentment had exhausted me, and I hated feeling bitter toward the closest family member I had left.

"I owe you an apology," she began.

"Not really," I said, because it was true. Her apologies were due to her daughter, not to me.

"Nonetheless, you're going to listen to me while I make it." She insisted with the same high-handedness she tended to use with others. She clasped her hands in her lap so tightly that her knuckles turned white. Then she added a soft, uncharacteristic "Please."

I was so surprised, I blinked and nodded.

Tilly took a deep breath. "I'm sorry I didn't respond when you first reached out to me about your mother."

I opened my mouth to thank her, but she shook her head and continued, "Let me finish. Honest emotional discussions are a pain in the ass, which is why I've gone far too long without saying all I need to say." She drew herself up slightly. "I know I told you and your mother that I was busy with family things when you first reached out me. That I'd been nervous and conflicted about getting in contact with her."

I nodded.

"Neither of those things was a lie. And Kelly chose to believe they were the whole truth, because she was kind and generous like her father." Her eyes met mine. "But I know that those reasons never flew with you."

I let out a breath. Finally, she was going to get real with me. "No. They didn't."

"Because you're more like me than is ever going to be comfortable for either of us, Miller Hobbs." She gave me a half-smile, and then she sighed. "The truth is, I hesitated because I was terrified. More terrified than I could remember being since the day I brought your mother into the world. For two reasons." She cleared her throat. "First, I was scared of telling Harold. You see… he and I were together before he went to college. And when I found out I was pregnant after he'd left for Princeton, I had to make a hard decision… change the course of his life or let both of them go. We all know the decision I made, but when I made it, I never in a million years expected I'd meet Harold again or that he would be a political celebrity of sorts. And I certainly didn't expect to hear from the baby I'd given up."

She took a moment to gather her words before continuing. "Confirming to the world that Harold and I had a child out of wedlock had consequences beyond just me. It affected his reputation, his legacy, the reputation and legacy of his son. Because of them, this was never going to be a simple reunion of Kelly with her birth parents. She would be thrown into the spotlight on an international stage whether she liked it or not. And she was."

Tilly spoke the truth. When the story had come out, reporters had swarmed to our doors, begging and harassing. Harry had been forced to arrange private security just so we could come and go without being bombarded.

She kept going. "The idea that I would introduce that kind of scrutiny onto her in her final days was abhorrent to me. But I

122

also knew Harold deserved to know, that he deserved to make his own choice finally." Tilly paused and finally shrugged. "Once he insisted on seeing her, that was that. I couldn't save her—or you—from what happened next with the reporters."

I held back from snapping at her by taking a breath first. "She didn't care. Not for a second. It was all worth it to her for a chance to meet you and get some closure. That was *her* choice."

Tilly nodded slowly and ran her finger around the wedding band on her opposite hand. "But the need to protect people isn't an easy thing to turn off, is it?"

I opened my mouth, then shut it again. "No," I admitted softly. "Not for me either. Especially protecting my mom."

She gave me a small, conspiratorial smile, and I blew out a breath. She and I really were more alike than I'd thought.

"But even after your grandfather knew about your mom," Tilly went on, "I still couldn't bring myself to go see her. Because I was still terrified."

I scowled. "Of what? She didn't want anything from you, you know. She just wanted to get to know you—"

"Exactly!" Tilly exclaimed, throwing her hands up and letting them flop back down into her lap. "Jeez, Louise, can you even imagine? Kelly was my girl, Miller. My precious daughter. My one and only child. I saw her for precisely one minute after she was born. That's all the time they gave me. For the sixty shortest seconds ever recorded, I held this tiny, fragile being who was part me and part Harold, and I loved her so much, so goddamn much, that I knew I'd move mountains and slay dragons if she needed me to. It killed me that the thing she needed from me most was to let her go. But I never stopped loving her. Not for a single moment of her existence. And I never will. Not for a single moment of *mine*."

She swallowed hard, clenched her hands into fists, and went on firmly, "I always tried to be the sort of person she'd be proud of, if she ever came looking for me. To be a good person… But you don't get to be my age without causing the occasional scandal, or breaking some hearts, or stirring up trouble. So I wondered, what if I met her and she didn't like me? What if she regretted getting in touch with me at all? What if she'd built me up to be someone sweet and shy and motherly, the kind of person I've never been in my life, and I disappointed her?" Tilly shook her head. "I tell you, I haven't given a crap what anyone thought about me since the Nixon administration, but suddenly, I was shaking in my boots. And to top it all off, all I could think was... Tilly, if you fell in love with your daughter that much in sixty seconds. If it was that hard to give her up as a baby, how much harder will it be to lose her now?"

Oh.

Oh, god.

I closed my eyes as the sweet ache of her words flowed through me.

"I know you think that was selfish, Miller, and it was. *I* was. I don't expect you to forgive me for it. But you need to know that it wasn't because I didn't care about your mother or you. It was because I loved you both so much."

My eyes flew open, and I met Tilly's watery gaze. "Thank you," I croaked. "For telling me that." I hesitated for only a second before I shared, "One of the hardest things about losing her has been this feeling that no one misses her as much as I do. That I have to carry her memory alone—"

"You don't, sweetheart. I promise, you don't." Tilly's face crumpled, and my heart suddenly almost broke for her. "I miss her every single day. And I regret the memories I could have made with her and didn't." She straightened in her seat and firmed her jaw stubbornly, the same way my mom used to. "Which is why I'm determined not to make the same mistake with you. You will never, ever be alone. Not as long as I am alive and not as long as anyone who ever loved me is alive to carry on my wishes. You're the most important person on this earth to me."

I blinked in shock. "I am? But you don't even—"

"Know you? Please." Tilly waved a hand. "I'm aware that I don't know you as well as I'd like to, but I know plenty, remember? I make it my business to know all kinds of things about the people I love. For example, I know you're not thrilled to be living in Monterey, but you don't think you have options. I know you've been too damn proud to accept help from me or your grandfather, so you've been slaving away for a bunch of tooth-torturers—and honestly, Miller, you have to wonder what kind of shady dental professionals purposely set up shop in a strip mall between a penny candy store and a boxing school." Her lips tipped up in a crafty smile. "I know you deserve the love of a good man… and I'm pretty sure you've found it."

I shook my head. "Wait. Just… just wait a darn minute." I scooted around the subject of Darius like it was a live wire. "How in the world do you know that Happy Teeth is located in a — Oh my god." I clapped a hand over my eyes. "Ella Marian was wearing a Happy Teeth T-shirt today, wasn't she?"

I'd noticed it earlier in the day but hadn't stopped to wonder why she was wearing it. I was so used to seeing the company logo, I hadn't realized how out of place it was here, on a child who didn't live anywhere near a Happy Teeth location.

Tilly inclined her head. "I believe Blue and Tristan were in your area when the kids were due for checkups."

She was lying. Blue and Tristan's kids weren't old enough for braces, and I remembered those shirts had only been available in the original Monterey location closest to Mom's house. Tilly had to have stopped by the office to see me, not realizing I mostly worked from home.

I lifted an eyebrow—a move I stole directly from Tilly herself—and she snorted.

"Fine, fine. You wanna talk turkey? I've been all up in your grill for months," she admitted. "I had to find ways to help you, didn't I, since you're stubborn as a goat?"

"I think you mean as stubborn as my grandmother." Other pieces began falling into place. "Mom's funeral expenses weren't paid for by her old boss, were they?" I demanded, glaring at her. "That was you! And her…" My throat clogged. "And her wish of being buried by the lake. You made that happen. Thank you."

Tilly scoffed. "Don't talk to me about money. I've got more than I'll ever need. If you weren't so stubborn, I wouldn't have had to work so hard behind your back. It makes me feel very

125

useless when you won't let me help my own… daughter." Her voice cracked on the last word, and I reached out to grab her hands. "Or my grandson."

"She didn't want your money, and neither do I," I said gently but firmly. "And I don't want you going behind my back to do things. For example, telling Mikey I'm happy in Monterey so he wouldn't offer me a job in Aster Valley—"

She sighed. "Yes, alright. I knew I was pushing my luck even while I was doing it. But I didn't want you to move away from your family, from Harold and me, before we really got to know you. Especially if you were only moving because of your finances." She flashed me that cunning smile again. "But you wouldn't be moving for that reason anymore, would you? You'd be moving for *lurve*. Because you found yourself a man with a big, Greek—"

"Nope. *Nooope*." I shook my head vehemently. "I am not discussing Darius or his big, Greek *anything* with you. Ever."

Tilly clapped a hand to her chest. "I meant his bakery, Miller," she said, all innocent horror. "His big, Greek *bakery*."

I sputtered with laughter. "You did not!"

"Didn't I?" Her eyes sparkled, and I felt a wave of affection for her crash over me.

She wasn't perfect, just like my mom hadn't been perfect, but she loved every bit as fiercely. A man could do a whole lot worse than to have someone like Tilly Marian in his court.

"I owe you an apology, too," I admitted. "I've been blaming you for things without even trying to see your side. My mom would be so annoyed at me."

Tilly shrugged. "It's easier to be angry than sad. Nobody understands that like I do. And if you can't be real with your family, when can you? Besides, you were right earlier when you told Simone I was strong enough to handle it. I'm tough."

But was she, really? I didn't think she was nearly as strong as she liked to pretend she was.

"I love you. I want you in my life for as long as possible. And when I thought you'd gotten yourself in trouble the other day at the sheriff's office, I was scared to death. I don't know what was

126

worse: the fear of you going to jail or the fear of you getting into a sleigh accident."

"Oh, that." She waved her hand. "I'm like a cat. I always land on my feet."

That pissed me off. "Bullshit! You're not immortal any more than my mom was. It was reckless and thoughtless. Do you have any idea how much Harry worries about you? What his face looked like when the call came in that you'd been arrested? Do you know how that made me feel?"

"Well, I..." She blinked, startled. "No?"

I stood up and began to pace. "All those people out there in that tent love you. They rely on you. So you can't just go off half-cocked and do whatever the hell you want like it's all some big joke."

"Nonsense," she spluttered. "They understand. They're used to me. And Harry knows I—"

"You know why Harry doesn't say anything?" I didn't wait for her to answer. "Because he's terrified you'll leave him if he pushes back in any way. And you know why? Because you've made it very clear to the people around you that it's your way or the highway."

She looked indignant, and part of me felt guilty for it. I bit my tongue against an apology.

"Everyone I've ever loved is gone, and there you are taking unnecessary risks with your life for what? A few minutes of fun? A prank?" I turned and gave her an accusing glare. "How would you like it if I did something so risky? Or if Harry did?"

"I had no idea you felt that way," she said stiffly, lifting her chin.

"I do," I said, deflating. "And so does Blue. And so does Simone. And Thomas and Rebecca. And Grandpa."

Tilly looked around the room before finally setting her eyes back on me. "I'm not used to this. To having to talk about... *feelings*." She said the last word as if it disgusted her. As if she had to pick its dirty carcass up between two fingers and dispose of it quickly.

I couldn't hold back a snort-laugh. Both of us looked at each other in shock at the incongruent sound.

"You started it," I said with a grin. "Besides, as my grandmother likes to say, 'If you can't be real with family, when can you be?'"

Tilly sniffed and tried to look annoyed but couldn't quite manage it. "Is this what having a grandson around is going to be like?" she demanded. "Having someone call me on my bullshit all the time, and refuse to let me interfere in his life even when I know better than he does, and force me to slow down and take care of myself?"

I pretended to think about this for half a second. "If the grandson is me, then... yes."

She held my gaze unflinchingly and nodded once. "Okay, then. I accept."

I felt a slow warmth spread through my chest, soothing some of the hollow, burned-out places that had been ravaged by grief. Nothing would ever, *ever* make me stop missing my mom. But I didn't have to carry that burden alone.

"Just to be clear, you're renouncing your life of horse thievery?" I demanded, squatting down so I could look her in the eye. "No more stolen draft horses?"

Tilly pursed her lips and muttered something under her breath in a mournful tone that sounded an awful lot like "My grandson is the fun police," but she nodded.

"I will pay more attention to my safety," she promised. "Though, in my defense, when a woman's best friend dares her to do a thing, she has little choice but to comply."

I rolled my eyes. "If Granny jumped off a bridge, would you jump, too?"

"Of course not," she said primly. Then she ruined it by continuing. "Someone has to stay behind to shoot the video for social media, after all, and Irene's worse at cinematography than at cards."

I snorted, and her haughty front softened as she lifted a hand to cup my cheek. "You only get one shot at this life, Miller. And I already have enough regrets to last a lifetime. I don't want to sit in some quiet room somewhere and wait out the rest of my days peacefully. I want to take chances and enjoy every minute of the adventure, even if that has consequences."

I dropped my chin to my chest and groaned. "My grandmother just YOLO'd me."

She fussed with her cuffs, but I could see the hint of a smile on her lips. "I never did get the hang of those things. Damned string kept tangling around my fingers."

"That's a yo-yo," I corrected.

She shot me a wink, and I groaned again.

"Sucka," she said, standing up. "Since *you only live once*, I would ask you to escort me back to the tent for dessert, but I fear you have another place to be."

"I don't have anywhere else to be," I said, standing and holding out my arm for her. She swatted it away.

"Really? Because I feel like a certain someone might be waiting to wish you a Merry Christmas. Someone who's been endowed with a magnificent, perfectly sculpted—"

"Tilly," I said in a warning voice.

"—head of *hair*," she finished guilelessly. "Honestly, Miller."

I shook my head. She was incorrigible. "Pretty sure Darius left." I tried not to think about how he must have felt seeing me break down in the middle of the party. "I doubt he's waiting for me."

"Care to make a wager on that? Because I'd be willing to bet that Darius Grant has been waiting a long, long time for you. And he'll keep waiting until you're ready."

My cheeks went hot. "I... He doesn't... I'm not sure... We only met a few days ago."

"But you and I know better than to waste time, don't we?"

I blew out a breath. "Yeah."

"That's why you're going to go find him and make the most of your time together. And if he turns out to be as special to you as it seems... well, then... you'll have to move here to be with him. And I suppose I'll just have to purchase a plane and make frequent use of the private airport here. It will lessen your inheritance, of course, but needs must. I certainly can't do the trip in

129

that dreadful recreation vehicle. Especially now that Dante and AJ have… personalized it, shall we say."

"Inheritance?" I squeaked. "No. My mother—"

"Was very much aware that you would be my sole heir after she passed." Tilly's tone dared me to object. "I believe it gave her some comfort to know that you'd be well taken care of as my heir. And even more that you'd be well loved."

"Heir?" I squeaked again.

I stared at her until she reached out a long finger and lifted my chin. "Close the shock flap, darling boy. Who else would it be? Now, skedaddle. I expect you boys to be here for Christmas morning present-opening, yes?"

"Yes, ma'am," I replied automatically.

"Good. Because I bought you a Ferrari, and I can't wait to see the look on your face when you open it."

I nearly tripped over a toy dump truck. "You *what?*"

"Relax. I'm just kidding. I knew you'd never accept something so gauche."

As we parted ways farther down the hallway, I could have sworn I heard her say, "You know what's not gauche? Mutual funds and real estate holdings. They're a bitch to wrap, though…"

I turned to stare at her, dumbfounded, and she laughed exuberantly. "Give Darius my love. Hopefully for Christmas he'll slip you some of his hot, yummy Greek—"

"Pastries?" I guessed, refusing to fall for her joke again.

She wrinkled her nose. "Well, I was thinking dick, but you do you, boo."

I ignored her and continued on my way, grabbing the keys to Mikey's SUV without stopping to ask permission. He'd already given me blanket permission to borrow it, and I knew he and Tiller had two other vehicles they could use if something came up.

The drive down the mountain was filled with promise. I turned on the radio just in time to hear my mother's favorite Christmas carol. The sounds of "Joy to the World" filled the vehicle and made me smile. I spent the rest of the drive through town and up the other side of the valley singing at the top of my lungs.

When I pulled up outside of Darius's house, I parked beside his truck and stared into the trees.

I felt like I was on the cusp of one of those important, pivotal moments, the kind that split one's life into Before and After. I'd had many of these moments in my life up till now, and, in fact, they littered my past like small rock cairns along a winding path through the wilderness.

When I stepped out of the SUV and turned toward the house, I got the strong feeling this time was different.

This wasn't a small rock cairn. It was a large, beautiful neon sign pointing in bright, beautiful lights toward a new beginning.

YOLO indeed.

14

DARIUS

When the doorbell rang, I wasn't surprised. I only wondered which Miller would be on the other side. Would it be the heartbroken man crushed by his strong-willed grandmother or a happy one who'd worked some things out?

I didn't have time to gauge his expression because as soon as I opened the door, he tackled me to the floor.

"Sorry, sorry!" he said against my lips. "Need this. Need you. Want you."

We lay in a tangled heap on the rug in the entryway with crystalline ice flakes floating around us through the open door. Miller's kisses were warm and plentiful, and I laughed in response to his uncontrolled enthusiasm.

"Merry Christmas to me," I said before rolling over him and deepening the kiss.

We made out like teenagers until my body reminded me I wasn't actually that young anymore. The hard floor under the rug and the frigid air from outside conspired to put an end to the delicious interlude.

"Sofa," I said, yanking my lips off the hot skin of his neck. I stood up and threw the door closed before yanking him up by the hand.

Miller's blond hair, normally perfectly styled, was in a messy swirl from where my hands had been, and his lips were wet and dark pink. His eyes were bright and happy, which was all I needed to see before sharing a wide smile with him.

"I take it things went okay after I left?"

Miller kept a tight grip on my hand and pulled me toward the sofa, where my blanket nest and glass of wine revealed the spot I'd been in when he'd arrived. He sat in the corner of the sofa and pulled me down next to him. We both turned to face each other, and I took a moment to throw the blanket over his legs and offer him a sip of my wine.

He took the glass and tipped it back for a healthy swallow. The light from the fireplace made him look like a golden boy.

"You're so beautiful," I murmured, letting my private thoughts escape.

He studied me while he took another sip. Then he set the glass back down on the side table and reached for my face with his hands. "Am I the only one feeling this?" he whispered. "Tell me I'm not alone in thinking there's something here."

I reached up and covered his hands with mine. "Not alone. And never will be again if I have anything to say about it."

It was a leap of faith. I knew that. But it was one my gut screamed at me to take.

"Darius," he breathed.

I leaned in and kissed him tenderly. My stomach tightened while my chest swelled. He was mine. I knew better than to predict the future, but right now, he was mine.

And that was all I needed.

Instead of asking him how things had gone with Tilly, I set those thoughts aside and continued kissing him, pressing him back into the arm of the sofa until he was prone beneath me.

He seemed to want this, want me, and I wasn't in a position to argue. There would be time enough later to talk through everything else. But for now, it was Miller and me, the crackling fire, the low melody of a jazz holiday playlist on the speakers, and the peaceful, silent night outside the wall of windows.

I took my time undressing him, kissing every inch of skin that was revealed like I was unwrapping the best Christmas present I'd ever received, until he suddenly decided to turn the tables. We slipped down onto the rug between the sofa and the fireplace, and he pushed me onto my back.

"My turn," he said. His sparkling eyes were full of playful mischief, and he was so relaxed and happy, it seemed like he'd ditched the heavy weight that had been on his shoulders before arriving here.

I watched him explore my chest and stomach with hands, lips, and nipping teeth. My dick throbbed with need until he put his hand around it and sucked it down. My brain blinked out as I arched back and groaned. He felt so damned good.

"Don't stop," I begged.

As he blew me, his free hand roamed over my chest until he found my nipple and tweaked it between his fingers. I grabbed his wrist to keep it there.

The sight of Miller Hobbs between my bent knees was incredibly hot. Watching his lips stretch around my cock made me wonder how much longer I could make it before pulsing hot and fast down his throat.

"Miller," I warned in a rough, broken gasp. "Baby, I can't…"

He moved a hand down to fondle my balls and took me deeper until my dick slid into his throat. There was no holding on after that. I grabbed his head and held on through the throbbing release as I let out a long groan of pleasure. As soon as he swallowed my release, Miller scrambled up to straddle my hips as he jacked himself.

"Oh god," I breathed, trying to steady my heart rate, which was nearly impossible while gorgeous Miller was naked and writhing on top of me with his thick cock in his hand. My own spent cock twitched half-heartedly, trying valiantly to rally as my breath heaved in and out. I had the vague notion that this sexy man was going to kill me… and couldn't think of a better way to go. "Fuck, baby."

I reached out and ran my hands possessively up his inner thighs. The curve of his muscles, the light-colored hair on his legs, the tightening of his sac, the sounds he made as his hand brought him to completion—every single part of him was bewitching. My heart thundered like I was chasing my own orgasm again.

"Come for me," I urged. "Want to see you come all over me. You're so damned sexy. Miller, please."

His glassy eyes locked on mine as he finally reached orgasm. The long, low sound out of his throat made my stomach tighten as I felt the first warm splatter of his release hit my skin.

His release seemed to last forever, and he never took his eyes away from mine. My chest squeezed from the intimacy of the moment. How was it possible to feel this way so quickly?

No more words fell between us as he lowered himself on top of me and lay quietly on my chest. My hands moved over the damp skin of his back and into his hair as our breathing finally settled into a peaceful rhythm. It wasn't until the cum drying between us began to itch that we finally stirred from the impromptu embrace.

"Let's shower," I suggested. "And then I want to feed you."

The shower turned into a long, lazy kissing session under the hot spray until I heard poor Miller's stomach growl. I knew he hadn't eaten much at dinner, so I quickly finished washing us and drying us both before finding a pair of soft flannel pajama bottoms and a sweatshirt for him to wear and donning a similar combo myself.

When we made our way back out into the main part of the house, I turned on the kitchen lights and began rummaging through the fridge. "What are you in the mood for?"

I was expecting him to demur with his usual polite sweetness, so when he said, "Pizza," with such excitement, it made me laugh in surprise.

"Pizza it is, then," I said, grabbing the dough I'd made a couple of days ago when I'd fully expected to be spending Christmas Eve alone.

Miller took a seat on one of the stools at the kitchen island. "Ever since you told me about making homemade pizza, I've wanted to try it."

I pulled out the ingredients for the sauce, as well as fresh mozzarella, basil, and spicy salami. "It's easier than you think if you use a food processor for the dough. And then I can mix up the sauce and toppings each night. It's my version of making a sandwich, I guess."

He smiled and shook his head. "Only a professional chef would say making pizza from scratch is like slapping together a sandwich."

I preheated the oven before chucking the ingredients for the sauce into my food processor. While it pureed, I peeled off some stringy pieces of the cheese to hand to him for a pre-pizza snack and then poured him a glass of wine.

"Tell me about Tilly," I said as I began stretching out the dough with floured hands.

Miller took a sip of wine first before setting the glass down and twisting the stem between his fingers. "She makes a good scapegoat," he confessed.

"What do you mean?" I asked, even though I was pretty sure what he was going to say.

"I was blaming her for everything because it was easier than facing my first Christmas without my mom." He let out a breath. "Much easier to get angry at Tilly than angry at my mother for leaving me alone."

I stayed quiet while he processed his thoughts.

"I realized on the drive over here that I've been feeling guilty and… and angry." He shrugged. "Being around all of my new Marian and Wilde cousins… it made me wish my mom hadn't stopped at one child. I realized how much richer my life would have been with siblings." He held up a hand. "And before you say that's not fair, I know. She did the best she could, and just because I might have wanted siblings doesn't mean she was even able to or interested in having more kids. I felt guilty for wishing that. So much that I didn't even want to acknowledge it to myself."

"You're allowed to wish things were different," I suggested.

"I know, but it's not fair to be angry at her. Nor is it necessary." He sighed. "And deep down, I'm also angry as hell that she left me. As much as my brain knows it wasn't her fault, that she fought to live with everything she had, my heart is still having trouble understanding. But then I felt guilty for that, too. Tilly and I talked about it, though, and that helped. A lot."

I finished stretching out the dough and laid it down on the pizza peel before wiping my hands and reaching across to take one of his hands in mine. I leaned forward and kissed it since I couldn't reach any other part of him. "I know you know this, but those feelings are completely normal and to be expected. Anger is part of grief."

"Thank you for saying that. It's just... This big family is so full of life, Darius. It's not fair that she missed the chance to be a part of it. She would have fit in with these weirdos so much better than I do."

I paused in the act of ladling marinara sauce to give him a curious glance. "Do you really think that?"

"Sure. She would have loved all of the personalities and the crowds of..." He stopped and frowned. "Hmm. Actually, she wouldn't have enjoyed this setting at all. She hated crowds of noisy people."

"And I think you're underestimating yourself," I suggested gently. "You might not be comfortable around strangers, but it's a different story around people who accept you and care about you."

"I think you might be right." He seemed to realize what he'd just agreed to. "Wait. You think they... yeah. Yes. They do." Miller beamed at me. "I love those weirdos."

"Uh-huh." I returned his smile. "Other than being pissed at Tilly, you seemed pretty comfortable around everyone tonight. Not overwhelmed at all."

He sat up a little straighter. "You're right. And even when I was upset at Tilly, everyone was kind and gracious."

"Because they accept you for who you are, not just as Tilly's grandson. They love you, too, you know. Every single person at that table tonight was concerned about you. They want you to be happy, Miller. No matter what that looks like. Tilly, too. She cares about you a lot."

He nodded. "I know that now. And I understand why Tilly

hesitated when my mom wanted to meet her. She was scared, and she let that hold her back. And she regrets that now."

I finished putting the toppings on the pizza before sliding it into the oven. Then I made my way around the kitchen island and stepped between his legs. I took his hands in mine.

"Someone else at that table tonight cares about you an awful lot, too," I said softly.

His eyes danced. "Was it Saint Wilde? Because he's hot as hell. And we're not blood related. Also? His husband is tiny. I could probably take him in an arm wrestle."

I let go of one of his hands and poked him in the chest. "No. And now that cocky bastard is dead to me."

Miller gripped my poking hand and brought it to his lips, where he pressed a soft kiss to my fingertip. "Was it my second choice? The Greek god with the sexy man bun and all the gorgeous ink that makes my dick hard?"

I stepped closer to him and leaned in to press my lips at the very edge of his. "Mm. Am I at least a *close* second?" I murmured before moving my lips across his cheek to his ear.

"Really close," he breathed as I took his earlobe between my teeth. "Like… maybe new first choice kind of close."

I nibbled on his ear and neck before returning my lips to his and taking my time with a lazy exploration of his mouth. When the oven timer buzzed, I jumped.

When we finally sat down on the sofa with our pizza, Miller returned to the subject of Tilly. "I told her to stop risking her life on stupid pranks like hijacking horse-drawn carriages."

I tried hard not to choke on my pizza. Imagining sweet Miller giving his grandmother the riot act made me laugh. "How did she take that?"

"She told me she'd take her safety more seriously," he said with a grin. "But we'll see what that actually looks like. She explained that she's doing her best to live her life out loud. I can't blame her." He paused before looking up at me from under his lashes. "She told me she loves me."

My heart squeezed with affection. "Of course she does. Who wouldn't?"

Our eyes stayed locked for a few beats as the words sat impatiently on my tongue.

Not yet.

It wasn't time, and this wasn't the night for it, no matter how confident I felt about the future. Sometime soon, and with complete abandon, I would say those three words to him for the first time of many. But in the meantime, I would be patient and—

Miller slid his plate onto the table and cleared his throat.

"I love you, Darius," he said softly.

My jaw dropped. "You—"

"Yeah, no, I know." He blushed all the way to his ears, just like he had the first day I'd met him, and waved a hand in the air. "We haven't known each other long enough for me to say that. I... I get it. I still don't know what kind of ice cream you like, or whether you talk during movies, or if you'll get impatient when I make you ride the same roller coaster six times in a row. I still don't know your thoughts on free-market capitalism, and you have no idea how much I utterly loathe certain classics of modern literature, and I have no idea if we brush with compatible toothpastes, but... but those things aren't *love* anyway." He broke off and took a nervous gulp of his wine before setting the glass back on the coffee table with a *clack*.

"Miller, I—"

He pressed a finger to my lips and shook his head. "Tilly's right. Emotions are a pain in the ass, so let me say this, okay?"

I nodded, even though staying quiet was really difficult. Happiness and relief were bubbling up inside my stomach, and I felt nearly buoyant.

"Love is... love is knowing someone will be the calm quiet in the middle of your storm. Love is someone who tucks a blanket around you and lets you sleep on his sofa. It's someone who never hesitates to make you feel wanted and supported... even when you flounce out of dinner because you need a minute to process something alone. And you're all of that for me."

"You didn't flounce," I couldn't help correcting gruffly.

One corner of Miller's lips tipped up in a momentary grin. "If my mom's death taught me anything, Darius, it's that life is short.

139

And messy. And fragile. And that you can't let fear of the unknown hold you back from enjoying the moments you're given. So, like, I don't expect you to say it back right away. Or maybe ever. Though, god, *that* would suck. But I just wanted you to know because... because it's Christmas. And you're the greatest gift I've ever been given. And holy shit, I couldn't be cheesier if I tried." He buried his face in his hands. "It's fine. I'm fine. How about some more pizza? I'll make it." He jumped up from the sofa like he was heading toward the kitchen.

Christ, I loved him. I wasn't sure what miracle had made this man stumble into my life, but I was never going to let him go.

"Are you done yet?" I demanded, grabbing him by the waist-band of his pants and pulling him down to sit beside me. I put my plate on the table next to his.

He nodded. "Oh yeah. Definitely. Yes. Don't worry. I just thought you should know, and now you do, and we can move on and —"

"I love you, too, Miller."

He turned his head and gaped at me. "You do?"

"More than I'd thought possible. You amaze me with your bravery and your resilience. And that's something I think *you* should know."

"Oh." Miller blinked. "Wow. That's... *wow*."

I laughed as I reached for him, pulling him onto my lap and wrapping my arms around him.

Miller leaned in and pressed a kiss to the underside of my jaw.

As the fire crackled and the snow began to fall outside, I wondered what our Christmas would look like next year. And the next.

When I'd sold my company and moved to a small town in Colorado, I'd never imagined I'd truly find the happiness I was looking for.

My yaya had a special word for all-consuming, uncontainable joy. *Kefi.*

Until this moment, I'd never truly understood the depth of the term.

And now I held it in my arms.

15

MILLER

Christmas morning with the Wildes and Marians defied description.

"What's happening in here?" Darius whispered against my ear as he followed me closely into the sunroom where chaos reigned.

"Santa came," I said, looking around at the mountains of torn wrapping paper, frayed ribbon, and empty toy packaging.

"He was obvs carrying quite a load," he murmured.

"I heard that," Granny said from her spot on an overstuffed chair nearby. "And it sounded dirty."

Irene sat primly on the edge of the same chair, taking pictures of the scene with her iPad. "Hush," she said without taking her eyes off the large tablet. "I'm taking videotape."

Darius sounded confused. "I only see a handful of kids, but there are enough toys here for—"

"Zzzzt!" Nico said, wagging a finger. "We do not judge the overpurchasing tendencies of others. Especially when it results in a killer wooden train set with bridges, rotating crossroads, and the cutest freaking conductor hat ever."

"Or anchor dildos," Cal added, waving a familiar toy in the air.

Darius's voice in my ear made me both shiver and laugh. "These children are growing up... differently."

"I'll have you know sex positivity is a gift," Granny stated defiantly.

Rebecca placed her hands over one of her granddaughter's ears. "Not sure it's a gift a three-year-old needs quite yet," she said under her breath.

Worth looked apologetic. "I told Cal to use the phrase 'toy' instead of... that other word."

"The D-word," Granny said with a cackle.

"But what if I said 'toy' and they asked to play with it?" Cal asked, horrified.

Rebecca sighed.

I turned to Darius. "I did warn you, you know. This is just... how they are."

He leaned in and gave me a sweet, lingering kiss. "Babe, you haven't met *my* family yet. Maybe by the time we've been together a few years, I'll start easing you into it one side at a time."

We'd stayed up most of the night sharing our daydreams and talking about the future. We hadn't come to any firm decisions on the specifics, but when I'd told Darius about my plan to move to Aster Valley, he'd reacted by rolling me over and kissing me, which had led to some extremely enthusiastic rimming and a dirty-talking frot session so hot I had to adjust myself in my jeans just remembering it, which seemed to indicate that Darius approved.

The knowledge that we would be together for years to come made me feel so excited and happy, there wasn't room for any guilt. I knew my mom would have wanted all of this for me—this family, this man, this excitement about the future—and I felt her presence surrounding me as I savored every moment.

"Can we start with the side that has the best food?" I teased.

"I'm afraid they both excel in that department. My Granny from Georgia makes brown sugar cornmeal waffles with sweet tea maple syrup. And Yaya makes spinach and feta tartlets. With that kind of background, I was pretty much genetically forced to go to culinary school."

After exchanging "Merry Christmases" with everyone, I kept a tight hold of Darius's hand as we moved farther into the room and found a place to sit on the floor near Hudson and Charlie. Charlie looked half-asleep with his head on Hudson's shoulder.

Tilly sat on the sofa nearby, so before sitting down, I leaned in and kissed her cheek. "Merry Christmas, Tilly," I said with a smile.

Her eyes searched mine before she let her smile widen. "You too, sweetheart. I hope you had a nice time last night and this young man gave you an amazing Christmas... *treat.*"

I straightened my shoulders. If I was doomed to hearing these innuendos from my grandmother for the next twenty years —and I seriously hoped I was—I was going to have to learn to respond better.

"Oh, he did," I told her with a firm nod, ignoring Charlie's snicker. "I've been very well... *treated.*" I lifted a challenging eyebrow at her, even as I felt my cheeks go hot.

Tilly's eyes widened in surprise, and then she burst out laughing. "Excellent, Miller," she said with an approving nod. "That's excellent."

Once I settled in next to Darius on the floor, I realized we hadn't arrived too late for most of the gift-giving. It seemed they'd let the little kids open some toys to help distract them while everyone else got settled with coffee and tried to shake off the early morning hour.

Simone looked adorably pregnant and half-asleep in her husband Joel's lap. His large, muscular arms held both her and their younger child while their older son played on the floor nearby with blocks. He looked as happy as a man could possibly be.

Blue was busy giving verbal instructions to Tristan as Tristan tried to assemble a complicated-looking toy. "Put that thing in the other thing," he said, pointing to a brightly colored plastic tab and a piece that looked like it had the matching slot.

Tristan didn't look up "That's what you said last night in the shower. I didn't listen to you then, and I'm not listening to you now," he muttered.

"Yeah, well... you owe me one. Telling me you're too tired because of... *Santa*," he hissed, "isn't exactly the way to a man's..." He looked around as if realizing he wasn't alone. "Heart."

Tristan shoved the tab into the slot with a satisfying *click* before beaming at his husband. "Shoved that bad boy in. What's next?"

Blue's ears turned pink before he busied himself with the instruction sheet, muttering, "You're killing me."

Mikey entered the room with two mugs of coffee and picked his way over to hand them to us. "Here you go." After we took the mugs from him, he pulled a couple of sheets of paper out of a pocket and handed them to me. "And here is some information about the marketing job we have open at the resort. Tilly said you'd be perfect for it, and we'd love to talk to you more about it if you're interested. On the other sheet is information for you on our chalets. We'd be happy to make one available to you at any time if you decide to come back and see..." He glanced at Darius with a knowing grin. "*Aster Valley* in the future." He winked at me.

My heart began to beat more rapidly. "I'd like that," I said, without daring to look at Darius.

We'd talked about our feelings and about me moving to Aster Valley, but we hadn't talked about where I'd be living when I got here. I didn't want him to feel pressured to move faster than he felt comfortable, and having someone in his space twenty-four seven might be moving a little fast for him, no matter how he felt about me.

Darius spoke up. "That's interesting because I was planning to give Miller a... *pamphlet* on the accommodations at Chez Grant, and I have to say, I believe it's a better fit for him than your lovely chalets."

Wait, what? I whipped my head toward him, but he only pulled me tighter against his side and went on, "Also, according to the internet, Happy Teeth's key performance indicators are top-notch, which I can only assume comes, in part, from Miller's marketing contributions. I'm sure you'd be in very good hands with Miller on your team."

My face ignited, but Mikey only grinned. "I'm afraid your recommendation carries as much weight as Tilly's. You're both way too biased."

Tiller came in and set a large tray of cut-up fruit and breakfast rolls on one of the tables. "You're one to talk," he said to Mikey. "You told me this morning we absolutely had to hire Miller to manage our marketing because he was, and I quote, 'really nice to be around.'"

Tilly huffed. "The man speaks the truth. There's no harm in that."

Charlie nodded without taking his head off Hudson's chest. "He really is. And so calm."

Hudson ran his fingers through Charlie's long red hair. "You wouldn't know calm if it bit you on your adorable Irish ass."

Charlie lifted his head to glare at Hudson. "Says a Wilde. *Pfft.*" Then he lay back down on Hudson and closed his eyes to enjoy the rest of his head massage.

King Wilde glanced over at us. "Wildes can be calm. I'm calm. I'm the king of calm, no pun intended. Steady under pressure is my special skill."

Falcon gave a begrudging nod. "It's true. Although the pun was absolutely intended. He does it all the time, and it's excruciating."

Lior met my eyes across the group and winked. "King. As if."

Felix elbowed him, Falcon laughed, and King groaned and murmured something about having received the name first.

I heard the nearly silent shutter release of a camera and turned to catch Teddy Marian sneaking a photo of Thomas and Rebecca curled up next to each other on one of the sofas with their heads together. Rebecca had someone's baby in her arm, and Thomas's thumb was gently stroking one of the baby's hands while he smiled and whispered something to Rebecca.

"They're disgusting," Pete said, rubbing his wife Ginger's

feet. "All that marital happiness should stay behind closed doors if you ask me."

Ginger scrolled through her phone as she enjoyed the foot massage. "Seriously. By the way, I arranged for someone to detail your car while we're gone. Merry Christmas," she told him without looking away from the phone.

He frowned. "You mean from when you and Noah spilled phallic glitter all over it after that bachelorette party? How is that my Christmas gift?"

She held out a bejeweled hand to him, still not looking away from the phone. "Also, you bought me a new sapphire ring for Christmas. It's freaking gorgeous. Thank you."

He took her hand and peered at it. "Huh. That is gorgeous. I have better taste than I thought."

"And a lower bank balance," she murmured under her breath. "But, like, way more head."

Pete grinned like a cat who'd eaten the canary. "Favorite. Ring. Ever."

"Thought so," Ginger said before hitting a button on the phone that made the *whoosh* sound of a sent email. "I also just forwarded you Green Day tickets. You're welcome."

Pete stared at her in awe. "You got me Green Day tickets? For real?"

She put her phone down and returned his smile. "Yeah. Had to murder a few people to get them, but it was worth it. You happy?"

Pete's chin began to wobble, and his eyes got suspiciously shiny. "You're the best wife I've ever had." He lunged for her and kissed her full on the mouth long enough to make their older daughters both gag and complain.

"Best one you ever *will* have, too," she said smugly.

So much for keeping the marital happiness behind closed doors.

"Who's Green Day?" Ammon asked, looking around the room for a hint.

"Newfangled shit," Jude said, tuning the guitar one of Pete and Ginger's girls had gotten. "Stick with the classics." He strummed a recognizable Rolling Stones riff before handing the instrument off to his niece.

Tilly made the throat-clearing noise that always indicated she was going to say something we all needed to shut up and listen to. I braced myself. It could be anything, honestly, and the sweet, sentimental feeling in the room didn't preclude irreverence.

"Shut the hell up," Granny barked. "The old lady wants to say something."

Tilly stood and glared over at her friend. Granny ignored her and snuggled Irene closer. "Go on."

Tilly made her way over to the tree, where she instructed the nearest Wilde cousin to hand her a specific gift. "Thank you," she said, taking the small box and turning toward me. "I have something special for Miller that I wanted you all to be here for."

"Oh god," Simone groaned under her breath. "Prepare yourself. Did anyone ever tell you the story about the Love Junk Christmas?"

Did I want to know? I wasn't so sure.

Jude covered his face with his hands. "I can't watch. If it's anything like that frozen vampire-shaped plug from last year—"

Derek covered his husband's mouth. "We don't speak of that. We had a deal."

"I just don't think any sex toy should be chocolate cream pie flavored, that's all," Jude said between his fingers. "It makes a horrible mess. And it's… indecent."

Beau Marian's face turned deep red. "Don't get me started on the vampire lube she sent us. Lube should never be a viscous red color. Ever."

Maverick shuddered. "Don't make me puke. Once was enough."

Tilly made a sharp hushing sound. "I'll have you know those are quality, American-made products, and half the proceeds of the Vampire Bites collection went to the Red Cross. I helped Noah come up with the slogan."

"'Give back while you give it up' was inspired," Granny said reverently. "I can see where Miller gets his marketing prowess."

Teddy snorted. "Using those products was like fucking people back to life, really."

Jamie smacked him. "I actually quite enjoyed the fangs. In fact, we still have a pair we —"

Thomas cleared his throat. "Let Tilly speak."

Rebecca let out a breath and muttered her gratitude.

Tilly ignored everyone and handed me the small gift. "For my beloved grandchild. May it be the beginning of a long life full of beautiful celebrations."

I put my hand on my heart. Here she was trying to be serious, and no one gave her a chance. "Thank you. That means so much to me."

I opened the wrapping carefully to reveal a stunning ornament. It looked like a disk of hand-blown glass with a splash of bright colors trapped inside. In colorful script on the front, it read, "I left my heart in Colorado."

Tears came to my eyes. I looked up at her. "How did you know? This is so special."

She nodded. "I told you I know you better than you think."

Granny muttered something about being disappointed in the boring gift, but Irene shushed her.

"Wait," Augie said from his spot on the floor nearby. "There's more on the back."

Suddenly, Tilly's kind expression turned mischievous. "Oh, did I forget to tell you? Hm."

I turned it over and read it out loud. "And my dick is there, too."

I blinked at the script as my brain tried processing what I'd just said.

Darius let out a huff of suppressed laughter. "Wow, you're right. You really do know him well, Tilly."

No one held back their reactions. The room filled with laughter. Tilly shot me a self-satisfied wink and returned to her seat.

I mouthed, "Dirty old woman," at her and then put my hand over my heart. "I love you."

Lior sighed. "That's better than the scepter ornament I got when I joined the family."

Felix rolled his eyes. "I keep telling you, that's not an ornament," he groaned before a blush stole up his neck. "And it's not
a scepter either."

Arthur shuddered but kept his mouth shut. Griff wasn't as
polite. "Hell no it's not. It's a KingMaker Deluxe with Court
Jester attachment. I helped her pick it out. After one use, you
won't be able to sit on your throne for at least a week."

Felix squeaked and buried his face in his cheesy Christmas
sweatshirt.

Darius leaned over and whispered in my ear. "I still can't
believe you're related to these people."

I glanced around the room at the motley collection of personalities. Every person in here carried a kind heart and a fierce
devotion to their family.

To *our* family.

"Me neither," I admitted softly. "But I'm starting to."

EPILOGUE
SEVERAL WEEKS LATER - DARIUS

"Take him down, motherfucker!" Tiller shouted at the television mounted high above the bar. Despite his own team's season being over, Tiller was still obviously invested in the outcome of whatever playoff game was being shown at Pie Hole.

Mikey muttered into his giant slice of pepperoni. "There are children here, dammit. Watch your mouth."

Tiller looked around as if realizing for the first time we weren't alone in the pizza restaurant. "Sorry," he said to a frowning mother nearby. He was famous enough and beautiful enough to make the woman blush and apologize back to him.

Tiller's friend Sam let out a deep bark of laughter that flustered the woman even more. I wondered if she realized both men were taken by other men. Sam's partner, Truman, was practically sitting on Sam's lap, but the woman wouldn't have been able to see that from where she sat with her family.

Mikey sighed before turning to Miller. "Did you have a chance to check out Tilly's new place on the way here? That guest bedroom on the third floor's got killer views, right?"

Miller's alcohol-glazed eyes flicked to mine, and I read his thoughts without him speaking a word. I shot him a wink.

"Yes," Miller answered politely, his voice a little slurred.

Not only had we stopped by to see his grandmother's new purchase, he and I may have already christened Tilly's place after we'd played a little drinking game called "Slurp the liquor off your boyfriend's body." It had gone so well, we'd had to get a ride to the pizza place.

"The house is beautiful, just like you said," Miller said earnestly. "But… it's bignormous. I can't imagine living there by my shelf."

Mikey hid his laugh behind another sip of beer. He wasn't as sober as he appeared either. He and his friend Julian had apparently been "testing" wines all day for a big wedding being held at the lodge on Valentine's Day. Julian was currently "resting his eyes" head down on the scarred wooden table next to Tiller.

I reached over and put my hand on Miller's thigh under the table. "No need for you to stay over there by yourself. In fact, there's no need for you to live *anywhere* by yourself. There's a perfectly serviceable spot for you at my house."

Truman's eyes widened. "Oh, Darius, I've heard about your house. It's a Catriona Ross, right? She designed the Aslan in Silverthorne. Have you seen it? It was in a magazine I saw at the dentist's office."

I nodded. "She's lovely. I heard she's designing a modern-concept ranch in Montana. I can't wait to see what she comes up with."

Sam's eyebrows dipped as he turned to Miller. "Wait, did I hear correctly? Your grandmother is moving to Aster Valley?"

Miller's body tensed. "She *is*?" He turned to me with big eyes. "Did you know that?"

"Babe," I said, reaching a thumb out to smooth the crease of worry between his eyes. "She's not moving here." To Sam, I explained, "She bought a big vacation home here so the Marians and Wildes can come visit. She wanted Miller to move in and live there while he got oottled in Aster Valley, but—"

"But I'm moving into the ski resort's new office," Miller interjected. "Mikey said I could."

Mikey and I exchanged a glance, and he winked.

Miller and I had talked about our living situation until I was blue in the face. I'd wanted him to move in with me, and I knew he wanted to also, but he'd insisted it was too soon.

Mikey had finally pulled me aside and said, "Nod and agree. We all know he's actually going to be living at your house. This just gives him plausible deniability."

He'd been right. Miller had happily brought almost everything he owned to my house "for the night" two weeks ago. The office sofa had yet to be turned into a bed even once.

Miller turned his heart-eyes from me to Truman. "It's across the street," he said with a proud smile. "Isn't that sweet?"

I clarified. "The ski resort rented the apartment above Mia and Mindy's shop as an office so they'd have a place in town for marketing and HR. It's a cute little setup."

Mikey smiled, and Truman clapped his hands and grinned at Miller. "Oh my gosh, that's perfect! I can meet you for lunch at Pim and Bill's sometime. You have to try their patty melt."

"I'll be too busy managing branding and marketing for the resort," Miller said proudly before turning to me. "Isn't that right? I'm going to brand and market the shit out of it."

Mikey offered him a fist bump, and I leaned in and kissed Miller's adorable mouth. "Pretty sure you'll still be able to make time for the odd patty melt. That's part of why you moved here, remember?"

"The patty melts aren't odd, I promise," Truman said earnestly. "But the portobello burger is, so maybe proceed with caution there."

Sam added a distracted nod. "Your lips to God's ears, cutie," he muttered before taking another sip of beer. He nearly choked on it. "Offensive pass interference! Did you see that? Motherfucker pushed off. They always let him get away with it. Prima donna bullshit."

He and Tiller shared a look of incredulous exasperation, as if there couldn't be anything worse in the world than an unfair call in football.

Mikey tapped his chin and pretended to look confused. "But isn't that what you do, baby? Don't you have a special move the media calls 'making Raine space'?"

Tiller's glare could have caught fire to the whole table. "Et tu, Brute?"

Sam and I both snorted while Mikey leaned forward and pulled Tiller to him for a kiss. "I love you. Don't ever make Raine space with me."

"Mpfh," Tiller grunted before turning back to the TV. I noticed he reached for Mikey's hand and held it firmly as he went back to watching the game.

Just then, Sheriff Declan Stone and Finn Heller came bustling in. "Sorry we're late," Finn said, pulling off his coat. "We were babysitting for a friend."

Miller did a double take and blinked at the sight of the famous actor.

The sheriff pulled out a chair for Finn before taking off his own coat and taking them both to a set of hooks by the door. When he returned, he asked Tiller for an update on the game. I noticed the woman who'd been impressed with Tiller and Sam earlier had caught a glimpse of Finn and nearly fallen off her chair.

She fumbled for her phone to sneak some photos, but Declan shot her a glare until she put her phone away.

Miller continued to stare at Finn. I decided to do the honors since everyone else was too drunk or distracted. "Miller Hobbs, this is Finn Heller. Finn, this is Miller. He's moving to Aster Valley and taking the marketing job at the ski resort."

Finn's famous grin was warm and welcoming. He reached out a hand to shake. "Welcome to Aster Valley. If you have any trouble with the law around these parts, let me know. I've got connections."

"Stop doing that," Declan grumbled without looking at him. "It's kind of illegal."

Finn rolled his eyes. "Arrest me."

Declan turned to face Finn. The heat in his eyes was unmistakable. "Remember what happened last time you said that?"

Finn tucked his bottom lip under his top teeth and breathed, "Sure do… *Sheriff*."

Miller's jaw dropped. "Did that sound as hot in real life as it sounded in my brain?" he whispered.

"Yup," Sam said. "Prettyyyyy much."

"No doubt," Mikey added with a nod.

Julian groaned and squeezed his eyes closed. "Everyone's doing it except for me."

Mikey reached around Tiller and rubbed Julian's back. "We can find you someone to do it with, sweetie. Believe it or not, Aster Valley has a super-active Grindr scene."

Tiller pulled himself away from the football game and tilted his head at Mikey. "Excuse me?"

Mikey ignored him. "When we first invited Sam to stay, we were going to arrange a bunch of fuck dates for him."

Now it was Truman's turn to balk. "*Excuse me?*"

Sam put his big muscular arm around the smaller man and pulled him close. "Didn't happen. Promise."

Miller leaned in and brushed his lips across my ear as he whispered loudly, "I'm gonna like it here. I love these guys. I mean not love, love, like I love you. But love. Like... love. You know?"

I bit my tongue against a laugh and nodded solemnly. "Yes. I know. And I'm happy you feel that way. They're great guys."

"Know who's a great guy?" Julian lamented sadly without picking his head up off his arms. "Parker Ellis. Great guy. The greatest. Except for the fact he's the worst. Like, the absolute worst. Like that meme. The worst. Ever."

Mikey mouthed the words "Straight best friend" at us. We all groaned.

Julian sighed. "I know, right? And he's getting married. On Valentine's Day. How cheesy is that? Super fucking cheesy. Spray Velveeta kind of cheese. The kind of cheese that gives all other cheese a bad name. And he doesn't even like shit like that, his girl—I mean, *fiancée* does."

Tiller reached out and patted Julian on the back. "Not true. Parker can be very cheesy. He once proposed to you on the Jumbotron at a Rockies game, remember?"

Miller and I swiveled our heads around to stare. "I thought he was straight?" Miller asked.

Julian flopped his hand in dismissal. "He is. That doesn't count. That was... that was just..." He sighed and sat up. "He proposed we take surfing lessons one summer in college. That's what he proposed. It wasn't marriage or anything."

"On the Jumbotron?" Truman asked. "That seems..."

"Weird as fuck?" Sam suggested. He nodded. "You'd have to know him. Parker is very fun-loving. But he's also thoughtful. One time, Julian had made a comment that no one had ever given him a prom-posal in high school. So Parker gave him a surf-posal on the Jumbotron."

Julian's eyes opened wider. "Wait, what? What?"

Tiller nodded. "Remember when you got upset that big prom gestures were something only the straight couples did? That really upset Parker. It's part of the reason he did the Jumbotron thing a couple of years later."

Julian's face crumpled, and he began to cry. "Oh, god. I love him. I love him so much."

Tiller and Sam exchanged a look. "Do something," Sam mouthed.

"Like what?" Tiller mouthed back.

"Julian, you should tell Parker how you feel," Mikey said, sounding exasperated. Clearly, this wasn't the first time they'd had this discussion.

"Can't," Julian moaned. "That'll screw everything up. Haven't you seen *My Best Friend's Wedding*?"

Truman sighed in exasperation. "Julian, life isn't a Julia Roberts movie."

"Doesn't matter," Julian insisted. "Going to wallow instead. Already bought a wallowing hole."

Mikey turned to Tiller and asked in a low voice, "What's a wallowing hole?"

"He bought a tiny cabin here when he realized he was going to be spending part of his time here working on legal stuff for the resort. I'm pretty sure he's planning on coming here after Parker's wedding to throw himself a pity party. Sam and I are trying to think of things to do to distract him."

I could see Mikey's mental machinations. He met my eyes. "Grindr fuck dates. We need to pre-arrange some hookups. Help him screw his way through the heartache."

I shook my head at the same time Miller nodded enthusiastically.

"No," Tiller said. "No interfering."

Truman put his fist under his chin. "I think Mikey's onto something."

"Stay out of it, sweetheart," Sam warned. "Julian's a grown man. He can figure out his own fucks."

I opened up my mouth to suggest putting a pin into the conversation until everyone was a little bit less shitfaced drunk, but Miller cut me off.

"I'm in the mood for cookie dick."

Everyone's heads swiveled around to our newest group member. "Come again?" I asked with a grin, knowing exactly what he was going to say in response.

"Don't mind if I do," he teased, pushing back from the table. "Because the first few times were worth repeating."

I stood up and threw some cash down on the table before grabbing our coats. "Sorry, guys. Duty calls."

As I grabbed my man and headed toward the door, I heard Julian ask what the hell cookie dick was.

Mikey answered through his laughter. "Let's just say it involves frosting and a lot of licking and leave it at that."

Julian groaned and lay back down on the table as everyone else laughed and continued enjoying their night out.

I squeezed Miller's hand and opened the door to the cold January air. The night was clear, and the moon shone brightly in the sky. Halfway up the mountain behind the town, I could see the light glinting off the steel of our house, where I'd left fresh flowers on the nightstand and Miller's favorite music playing softly on the house speakers.

This beautiful, kind man beside me deserved to be spoiled rotten, and I planned on taking my time tonight reminding every square inch of him how deeply he was loved and how grateful I was to be with him.

Miller wasn't alone in the world anymore, and he never would be again. He was a Marian now. And a Wilde.

But most importantly, he was *mine*. And we were going to build our future in Aster Valley.

Forever.

~

Want to find out what happens with heartbroken Julian at his BFF's upcoming wedding? Grab *Thick as Thieves* here.

If you haven't read any of the books in Aster Valley yet, grab Mikey and Tiller's story *Right as Raine* here.

FAMILY TREES AND WHO'S WHO

THE MARIAN FAMILY

Thomas and **Rebecca** Marian
Their children (oldest to youngest):
Pete, married to **Ginger**
Jamie (meets **Teddy** in *Taming Teddy*)
Blue (meets **Tristan** in *Borrowing Blue*)
Thad (dating Tristan's cousin **Sarah**)
Jude (meets **Derek** in *Jumping Jude*)
Simone (dating **Joel Healy**)
Maverick (meets **Beau** in *Moving Maverick*)
Griff (meets **Sam** in *Grounding Griffin*)
Dante (meets **AJ** in *Delivering Dante*)
Ammon (gets his story in *Made Marian Mixtape*)

Aunt Tilly - Thomas Marian's aunt

Non-Marians:
Granny - Tristan's grandmother
Irene - Granny's wife

Harold Cannon - Tilly's boyfriend (first appears in *Delivering Dante*)
Noah (appears with **Luke** in *A Very Marian Christmas*)
Ben (Griff's biological brother, meets **Reese** in *Made Mine*)
Gideon (Ammon's biological brother, appears in *Made Marian Mixtape*)

≈

THE WILDE FAMILY

Grandpa (Weston) and **Doc** (William "Liam") Wilde (get together in *Wilde Love*)
Their children:
Bill, Gina, Brenda, and Jacqueline

Bill married Shelby. Their children are:
Hudson (meets Charlie in *Hudson's Luck*)
West (meets Nico in *Facing West*)
MJ (meets Neckie in *His Saint*)
Saint (meets Augie in *His Saint*)
Otto (meets Seth in *Wilde Fire*)
King (meets Falcon in *King Me*)
Hallie
Winnie
Cal (meets Worth in *NautiCal*)
Sassy

Gina married Carmen. Their children are:
Quinn (*Made Marian Shorts*)
Max (bonus short called *Arthur & Max*)
Jason

Brenda married Hollis. Their children are:
Kathryn-Anne (Katie)
William-Weston (Web)
Jackson-Wyatt (Jack)

Jacqueline's child:
Felix (meets Lior in *Felix and the Prince*)

~

ASTER VALLEY CHARACTERS

Mikey and **Tiller** (*Right as Raine*)
Truman and **Sam** (*Sweet as Honey*)
Finn and **Declan** (*Hot as Heller*)
Julian (*Thick as Thieves*)

LETTER FROM LUCY

Dear Reader,

Thank you for reading *Forever Wilde in Aster Valley*.

Up next is Julian's story in *Thick as Thieves*. If you are new to Aster Valley, feel free to start with *Right as Raine* (Mikey and Tiller's story), but it's not necessary to read them in a particular order.

Please take a moment to write a review of this book on the retailer site where you purchased it and any other book site you use for reviews. Reviews can make all of the difference in helping a book show up in book searches.

Feel free to stop by www.LucyLennox.com and drop me a line or visit me on social media. To see inspiration photographs for all of my novels, visit my Pinterest boards.

Finally, I have a fantastic reader group on Facebook. Come join us for exclusive content, early cover reveals, hot pics, and a whole lotta fun. Lucy's Lair can be found here.

Happy reading!

Lucy

ABOUT LUCY LENNOX

Lucy Lennox is the USA Today bestselling creator of the best-selling Made Marian series, the Forever Wilde series, Aster Valley series, several standalone, and co-creator of the Twist of Fate Series with Sloane Kennedy and the After Oscar series with Molly Maddox. Born and raised in the southeast, she is finally putting good use to that English Lit degree.

Lucy enjoys naps, pizza, and procrastinating. She is married to someone who is better at math than romance but who makes her laugh every single day and is the best dancer in the history of ever.

She stays up way too late each night reading M/M romance because that stuff is impossible to put down.

For more information and to stay updated about future releases, please sign up for Lucy's author newsletter on her website.

~

Connect with Lucy on social media:
www.LucyLennox.com
Lucy@LucyLennox.com

WANT MORE?

Join Lucy's Lair
Get Lucy's New Release Alerts
Like Lucy on Facebook
Follow Lucy on BookBub
Follow Lucy on Amazon
Follow Lucy on Instagram
Follow Lucy on Pinterest

Other books by Lucy:
Made Marian Series
Forever Wilde Series
Aster Valley Series
Twist of Fate Series with Sloane Kennedy
After Oscar Series with Molly Maddox
Licking Thicket Series with May Archer
Virgin Flyer
Say You'll Be Nine
Hostile Takeover

Visit Lucy's website at www.LucyLennox.com for a comprehensive list of titles, audio samples, freebies, suggested reading order, and more!

Made in the USA
Middletown, DE
22 November 2021

53154934R00102